MILEPOST
67

MARIAN POTTER

Milepost 67

Illustrated by Sally Stiff

THE BODLEY HEAD
LONDON · SYDNEY · TORONTO

To the memory of

MY FATHER

I

'EVALINE, TAKE YOUR hands right out of that bread dough,' Mama ordered.

'But, why, Mama?' Evaline was wrist-deep in the sticky dough she had stirred up in the biscuit crock.

Evaline's brown eyes were big with surprise when she looked up at Mama, who seemed about to snatch the crock from her. 'I asked this morning if I could make supper bread, and you said, "Uh-huh," and kept right on working. Don't you remember?'

'I know it. I know it, Evaline,' Mama said quickly. 'But now that I see your arms rammed down in that dough I want you to stop, and no monkeying about it. Those little pipestem arms of yours! I'm afraid they'll break right off in the dough.'

Evaline bent her head so that her sister Opal wouldn't see her eyes full of tears. Opal, who was older and plumper than Evaline, stood by the kitchen cabinet and watched Evaline try to clean the dough from her hands.

Evaline tried hard to make her voice steady. 'My arms are strong, Mama. I can make bread.'

'Not for a while, not till you get some meat on you. It doesn't seem right somehow. You're such a cricket, and that's such a big batch of dough. Now wash your hands and go fill the chip basket for morning.'

With a clatter, Mama opened the round iron lid of the

cookstove and quickly poked split wood into the firebox. From the bench where she soaked her hands in the grey granite wash pan, Evaline watched the orange flames leap and light up her mother's face. The steam and heat of the kitchen made Mama's honey-coloured hair curl around her face no matter how tight she wound and pinned her long tresses to the top of her head.

Evaline dried her hands on the roller towel and took the chip basket from behind the cookstove. Now Opal was at the cabinet, flouring the breadboard. She grinned smugly at Evaline and said in a low voice that Mama couldn't hear, 'Pipestem arms.'

From the back door, Evaline gave Opal a look which she hoped was dark and threatening. Then she ran out to the woodpile.

Picking up bits of bark and splinters left from woodchopping was an ornery job, Evaline felt. It was fit only for little kids like Gertrude and Joe Junior, her younger sister and baby brother. Still it was nice to be outside. She was in no hurry to fill the big basket, which her grandfather had made out of white-oak splints.

Evaline sat on a chunk of stovewood. The warm spring sun felt so good on her back that, for a moment at least, she didn't want to move. She looked at her home, the small frame house where the Stevens family lived. The sun was turning its coarse, cracked yellow paint to a smooth gold. The railroad tracks that ran right in front of the house flashed silver in the sun. Evaline had always lived in the section house, because her father was foreman of a gang of men who kept a section of railroad track in repair. There were houses

6

like this for section foremen and their families every fifteen miles or so along the railroad right-of-way. All were painted bright yellow, daubed with the same brush used on the railroad depots that stood nearby.

Even thinking of living in a special place like the section house didn't make Evaline feel much happier. She was ten years old, but sometimes, people mistook her for nine or even eight. She was small for her age, but she could make bread. She'd watched her mother and her twelve-year-old sister, Opal, do it hundreds of times.

She looked up when she heard the yard gate click and saw Gertrude and Joe Junior following her to the woodpile. Gertrude was seven and Joe Junior only four. He held tightly to Gertrude's dress as if he was frightened, and Gertrude's grey eyes looked troubled. She had a basket too, much smaller than the chip basket.

'Evaline,' Gertrude said, 'do you know what we have to do? We've got to get the eggs out from under the hen that wants to set. Mama said so. She needs more eggs for supper.'

'Hen pecks,' Joe Junior said.

'Oh, there's nothing to it!' Evaline declared. 'You just go right up to the nest, throw your apron over the hen's head, reach under her, and get the eggs.'

'She ruffs up her feathers and squawks terrible,' Gertrude said. 'Grandpa Stevens said a setting hen might peck a person's eyes out.'

'Oh, she will not, no such silly thing,' Evaline said. 'Go on now. You know Mama's in a hurry.'

'I'm not so afraid the hen will peck me,' Gertrude

7

said. 'But I don't like to take the eggs away from her. She's figuring on having some little chicks; and now I have to rob her nest and make her mad.'

'You know hens don't figure anything, Gertrude, and we need the eggs.'

'Evaline, you do it; you get the eggs,' Gertrude pleaded.

'I'll do it if you and Joe Junior will fill up this chip basket—all the way up.'

Gertrude and Joe Junior began tossing chips into the basket as fast as they could, and Evaline started for the chicken house, swinging the egg basket in a circle round her.

Evaline had the three warm eggs in the basket before the setting hen had time to turn herself into a stabbing ball of feathery fury. She was coming out of the chicken house with them, when she heard a cowbell and knew that Wilbur Bates was driving the Bates's milk cow home along the dirt road that ran behind the section house.

She was glad she wasn't gathering chips when Wilbur came along. He never did baby jobs like that. He had a horse and rode out every evening to find April and drive her home to be milked.

The gentle Jersey plodded past, her bell clanging on her thick neck. Evaline watched Wilbur on his old horse, Tarpaper, make unnecessary forays into the buck-brush at the side of the road. He whooped and yelled at imaginary steers while April, driven only by habit, clanged on far ahead.

'Whoa-ho!' Wilbur commanded and reined up

8

beside the chicken yard fence. 'What are you doing, Evaline?'

'Oh, just taking eggs out from under a setting hen,' Evaline said. 'Mama doesn't want all the hens to set.'

'Setting hens are mighty mean,' Wilbur said.

'Don't scare me any,' Evaline declared. She looked intently at the boy on horseback. 'Wilbur, you know what you look most like?'

'No.'

'You look like a house afire. The sun is shining on your red hair, and it's standing up every which way; and your eyes are all squinted up like little upstairs blue windows; and your freckles are like a lot of little sparks; and——'

'That so? Well, watch me go like a house afire, then.'

Wilbur let out the reins, dug Tarpaper's sides with his heels, and yelled. The old black horse stretched out into Wilbur's favourite gait, a long lope, which he could keep up at least until he was out of Evaline's sight. By that time, they would be almost home and needing to slow down anyhow; for Wilbur's father thought Tarpaper was too old and stumbly to put into a fast rack.

Evaline watched red-clay mud fly up from Tarpaper's heels, then began to fly herself when Mama came to the back door and called, 'Where are those eggs?'

Evaline ran and gave the basket to Mama, who looked pleased and said, 'I'm mighty obliged to you, Evaline.'

Mama's voice was high and usually cheerful. She spoke quickly, like a jenny wren would speak, if it spoke, Evaline thought.

9

Evaline was helping Gertrude and Joe Junior carry the full basket of chips when they suddenly dropped their side, and out of the yard gate they ran. Evaline too heard the sound that made them run.

It was the handcar's iron wheels rattling on the rails and clicking every time they passed a rail joint. Up and down, up and down, the tired section gang pumped the handcar towards home and supper.

Evaline didn't intend to follow Gertrude and Joe Junior. They'd wait beside the track for Dad to come, then grab his dinner bucket and scrap over anything left in it. That was such little kid stuff. But suddenly she stopped struggling with the heavy chip basket and dashed through the yard and along the fine, grey stones beside the rails and crossties. She liked to run in this loose, coarse gravel which the railroad men called 'chat'.

The low western sun cast a shadow of a huge, lurching Evaline clear across the main-line track, the first sidetrack, and the second sidetrack. She bent her knees as she ran, so that the shadow-girl seemed to kick herself. She overtook Gertrude and Joe Junior in no time and stood with them near the toolhouse where the handcar was kept at night, and watched the men put it away.

As final job of the day, the gang had to lift the handcar from the main-line track over to the smaller, narrow-railed track that ran into the toolhouse. The men started off in different directions for their homes while Joe Stevens locked the toolhouse.

He held out his dinner bucket, and they all three grabbed it. Dad walked on without a word or a smile to his children. Talking would come later after rest and supper, Evaline knew. When he first came off the track, Joe Stevens was too weary for words.

Since Joe Junior was the youngest, he should be allowed to open the bucket, Evaline decreed. Joe Junior sat down on the chat and worked with the pail fasteners which opened suddenly and gave off a strong smell of onions from the bucket. Only a cold biscuit and some bacon rinds were left.

'Gertrude, you divide the biscuit. Then Joe Junior gets first pick.' Evaline found this method of division cut down squabbling time. She herself chewed on the salty bacon rinds and drank the bitter dregs from the coffee thermos. Under the thermos was tucked a little bunch of green blades that looked like coarse grass. Evaline sniffed it. It was wild onion, the first of the spring.

Dad washed at the bench when Evaline came back into the kitchen. He bent and brought handfuls of soapy water up over his face and neck. He sputtered and blew through his hands. From the tin case under the mirror, Dad took the comb. The grey at his temples became little grey wings, as he combed his hair.

Dad worked out-of-doors summer and winter, and his face was tanned and weather-beaten, all except his forehead, which was whiter than Joe Junior's. The fine pale skin of his forehead, always protected by his cap, looked as if it belonged to some other person.

'The chiggers are about to eat me alive,' Dad said. 'You wouldn't think they'd be out a-ready, after a fellow; but I believe they bite worse in the early spring.

The grass and weeds are full of them. They burrow right into the skin, and I can't even see the pesky devils. Evaline, get a toothpick and come out on the back porch in the good light.'

Dad, his faded denim overalls rolled above his knees, sat on a straight chair with his long legs on another, while Evaline searched for the minute red dots that meant chiggers. When she found one on Dad's leg, she deftly pricked it out with the end of the toothpick.

'It beats all how you can see them, Evaline. They'd itch so bad they'd keep me awake all night, if you didn't get them out.'

Mama and Opal were dishing up supper before Evaline had a chance to show Mama the wild green onions and asked if she could fix them for Dad's supper. Mama nodded. 'Just hurry up about it. Put a little grease in the smallest skillet. Take the stove lid off, so they will fry fast next to the fire. Then put them on Dad's scrambled eggs the way he likes them.'

Grandpa Stevens sat at one end of the table and began the supper by saying grace. He bent his head over his plate and mumbled the prayer. Evaline never knew what he said, but that didn't seem to matter much.

She sat on a bench along one side of the table with Gertrude and Joe Junior. On the other side sat Dad, Opal, and her big brother, Lester. Mama sat at the end opposite Grandpa Stevens.

Dad had started eating when Mama announced, 'Opal made the bread, Dad.'

'I never ate better.'

Opal grinned and sat up straighter. Evaline dreamed of the day Mama would say, just as matter-of-fact as you please, 'Evaline made the bread, Dad.' Then Opal's shrill voice cut into her dream.

'I had to finish what Evaline started,' Opal said. 'Mama was afraid her pipestem arms would break right off in the bread dough.'

Gertrude and Joe Junior giggled. Mama wasn't hurried now. She sat back in her chair and laughed. Dad had eaten enough to be in a good humour. His eyes began to twinkle, and he chuckled. Opal and Lester roared with laughter. Even Grandpa Stevens, who didn't even know what was funny, gave little 'H-mm-m's' that passed for laughter with him.

Evaline wished she were some place else. Tears of anger and shame rolled down her face. She slid off the bench and down under the table. The laughter died down a little; but when her small hand and thin arm came up from under the red checked cloth to get her plate to finish under the table, it started up again.

They'd laughed at her and made her mad, so Evaline thought no one, except Opal, would say much if she ran off after supper and left Opal to wash and dry dishes alone.

At the back door, she stopped to pet her black cat, Arnold. She crossed the road and ran below the nearby bluff. Then she went to the grapevine swing that no one else knew about. It was dusk when she came in from wandering around. Dad was in the front room, smoking his pipe.

'Just one thing I want to know,' he said. 'How did

those wild onions get from my dinner bucket on to my supper eggs?'

Evaline climbed on to his lap and hid her face against his shoulder. Then Joe Junior and Gertrude got jealous and came and pushed and shoved, so that she had to give up Dad's lap. But she clung to his hard shoulder.

Dad whispered to her, 'Lots of womenfolk can make bread. Nobody on the whole railroad division has eyes as good as you have for seeing chiggers, Evaline.'

By the time Evaline went to bed, she had almost forgotten how wretched she felt at suppertime. Opal was already asleep, breathing hard beside her, and Evaline knew that Gertrude was asleep on her cot. Evaline could hear Mama and Dad talking in the next room.

'If we had a cow, plenty of butter and rich cream, I know she'd pick right up, just in no time.'

Dad's deeper voice was harder to understand, but Evaline heard him say, 'There's nothing wrong with her eyesight or the way she can run. It's just her nature to be little and wiry that way.'

'Oh, she's quick, all right,' Mama said, 'always on the go—like a worm in hot ashes; but she wouldn't stand much in the way of a hard spell of sickness. If we had a cow, lots of fresh milk at every meal, well I just know she'd pick up. What Mrs Bates can spare isn't enough for all of us. As it is, she robs herself.'

'Cow'd be a lot of extra work, milking morning and night. We'd have to let her loose on the range. We've got no pasture, not even a shed for winter.'

'Oh, a cow'd be no trouble at all, Joe. Why, I'd do the milking, and the children would bring her up every night. Evaline goes with Wilbur Bates half the time to get their cow, anyway.'

'Milking on top of all you already have to do! You're almost run ragged, now! Besides, a good cow costs a lot to start with and to feed in winter.'

Evaline listened for Mama to answer, but it was Dad who spoke again. 'Besides that, it might be just something to get rid of if we move to a town where there is a high school. Lester ought to go on to high school now that he's finishing the eighth grade—a boy like him. Miss Mary Kyle says she has taught lots of boys, but never one that she would rather see go on to high school than Lester. If a job on a gang in a high school town comes up, I'm going to try to bid it in. Don't you think that's the thing to do, Nora?'

'It's hard to know what's best, Joe. You're foreman here, and in a high school town, most likely, you'd have to go back and be a labourer again. There'd be house rent in town, and your father wouldn't want to leave this little old town of Middling. I wouldn't be seeing my people so much. But I don't want to stand in the way of Lester's schooling, so I don't know——'

Her voice was drowned by the whistle of a steam locomotive. Suddenly there was a thundering roar, and a strong light shone into the girls' room. Opal and Gertrude did not stir, nor would Evaline later in the night when other fast trains went by a few feet from the room by the rails. With a rush, the train went past. Soon the lonely moan of the whistle died away.

Evaline could hear her father banking the heater fire still needed for chilly mornings. Then she heard nothing but the far-off baying of a farm dog, an occasional clang of April's bell, and the sweet cries of the spring peeper frogs.

Sometime in the night she awoke and heard a great sighing sound and voices almost beside her. She knew without looking out that a freight train was on the side-track, with a sighing engine giving off steam. The men of the train crew talked and joked out there in the night, just as if they were working in a store or on a section gang. Night must be very much like day to them, Evaline thought; she supposed it would be to any-one who worked right through night as most people did through day. She dozed as she tried to recognise some of the voices out there where lanterns bobbed. She was sound asleep when the fast train, for which the freight had taken siding, rushed past.

2

SCHOOL WAS OUT until fall. Evaline thought the April morning had a lucky-day feel. She'd had breakfast and wasn't exactly hungry; yet she wanted something to eat, something different and fresh. She'd been given a task, one she liked. She was to go to Clark's store for lard and coal oil. In one hand she carried a straight-sided tin bucket for the lard, and in the other a spouted can for coal oil. 'A little grease for us, and a little grease for the lamps,' Evaline half-chanted as she started down the railroad track, for the road was still a mess of muddy red clay.

Evaline could walk on the rails faster and farther without slipping off than anyone she knew. Still she must keep in practice. On the rail, she balanced herself with the lard bucket and the coal-oil can.

Beside the track, a flat post stood up like a white blade higher than Evaline's head. 'Milepost 67', it read. Evaline knew what it meant; Dad had told her. The railroad men had to know every mile of the track, and that post showed the exact distance from the big Union Station in St Louis. She had never been there; but some-day, when Mama decided they had proper clothes, the whole family was going. She thought of this trip as she balanced on towards the yellow depot with the sign 'Middling' on the gable.

The chat was wide round the depot. The roof hung

far out over the building. Hanging out farthest of all was a little bay window where Mr Bates, Wilbur's dad, who was the station agent, could work his telegraph keys and look up and down the track. In front of the bay window was a high pole that went up through a hole in the overhanging roof. High above the depot, atop the pole, was a semaphore. A ladder hugged the pole so that the semaphore could be reached for oiling and repairing. Although no one knew it except Wilbur Bates, once Evaline had climbed up that ladder through the roof opening, halfway to the semaphore.

As she came nearer the depot, she could see Mr Bates silhouetted at the telegraph desk. She could hear the steady clatter of the telegraph keys. Evaline went through the right-of-way gate to the track that ran behind the depot. This was the house track where cars were loaded. It was dull and sunken into the ground compared with the more important-looking main line. Evaline walked the house-track rail to the wide-open door of the depot freight room.

'Gee! Haw! Back up there, Blackie!' She heard Wilbur Bates playing teamster. The freight room door on the house-track side was high as a wagon from the ground to make freight loading easier. The floor began at Evaline's chin as she looked into the big, dusty room.

Wilbur and Orville Bates were both in the freight room. Orville, who was two years older and many times quieter than his brother, Wilbur, lay on a fat bag of coffee beans. His head was propped on his arm, and he was reading *Treasure Island*. He didn't look up from his book at Evaline. Wilbur had enclosed himself in a rectangle built of wooden tobacco boxes and nail kegs.

'Wilbur, I could hear you a mile off,' Evaline said. 'Is that all you've got to do, carry on like that?'

'No, I've got to hunt order hoops. Dad told me to. You can go along if you want to.' Wilbur had hoped Evaline would appear, for she was good at seeing order hoops along the right-of-way where grass was beginning to grow high.

'After I go to the store, we'll look on the way home,' Evaline said and started to run.

There wasn't much to Middling besides the depot. Across the road from it was a row of buildings: the post office, barber's shop, bank, and two general stores. A concrete walk ran in front of these buildings, but no one ever called it Main Street. It was just Middling. Back a little farther and up a hill were a few houses, the school, and the church. On the other side of the railroad tracks, level farm fields stretched to the river.

Evaline went to the store oftener than any of the other Stevens children. She got there and back quicker than anyone else. Gertrude and Joe Junior couldn't carry much. Sometimes they forgot what they were sent for; or Gertrude was too bashful to ask for something. Opal and even Lester always had something more important to do than run to the store.

Evaline liked Clark's store best. Mr Clark called her Miss Evalina and made a fuss over her. He talked to everyone else in the store, too, so that everyone felt he was getting attention. In this way, he could keep a store full of people from getting impatient.

As she waited for Mr Clark to bring the coal oil up

from the store cellar, Evaline looked hopefully along
the counter to see if there was anything different to eat
that she could tell Mama about. Maybe there would be
cabbage, or even some celery, as there had been at
Christmas. But there was no box of fresh food. There
was just the tobacco cutter on the counter, bins of dry
beans and peas, a barrel of crackers behind the counter,
and the tins of too-expensive canned peaches on the
shelves. Even the calendar was the same as ever except
for the year. The figures 1922 were big and red so you
couldn't miss them. But the picture at the top was un-
changed. It was the same stern-looking man in a white

coat and a round, white cap pointing to the same box of chicken louse powder.

When Mr Clark came puffing up from the cellar, he handed Evaline the oilcan. 'That screw cap that goes on the spout is missing, but that's all right. I reached into the bin and got a potato and stuck it on the spout so Miss Evalina won't get all sloshed up with coal oil.'

And she didn't as she hurried back to the depot.

She and Wilbur looked for order hoops between the depot and the section house. The wooden rings were as big as barrel hoops and had long handles with wire clamps on them. When Mr Bates or one of the telegraph operators who worked at night gave directions to a fast train crew, three copies of the order from the train dispatcher were made and clipped under the fasteners on the order hoops.

The station man stood near the track and held up the first hoop to the engineer, who caught it by thrusting his arm through the wooden ring. The second hoop was for the conductor, who leaned out between the cars to hook his copy, and finally the rear-end brakeman got his order hoop as he leaned from the steps of the last car. The trainmen took the tissue-paper messages from the fasteners and flung the hoops off the train, somewhere, along the right-of-way. When the number of hoops on the nail in the depot got low, Mr Bates gave Wilbur an order to go out along the track and bring some in.

Evaline liked to help and found the first hoop standing almost upright on its handle in a clump of dry weed stalks, and looking for the world, like one of them.

Wilbur stumbled over another one before he saw it. They both saw the third, for it was lying on a bed of fresh, green plants and showed up easily. As she picked it up, Evaline looked at the plants more closely.

'Say, that's curly dock. It's good for greens,' she said and began to pick the long, slender leaves.

'Do you eat those weeds?' Wilbur asked. 'I hate greens. I won't eat them.'

'Taste good in the spring,' Evaline said, 'after dry beans and more dry beans. Maybe I can get a mess of greens for Mama to fix. Cooked with a little piece of dry salt, and with some vinegar sprinkled on, greens are good. I'm hungry for a mess.'

'Nobody could make me eat them,' Wilbur asserted.

'You don't know what's good,' Evaline said. 'Say, look there. Even the poke-weed is up, and it's the best. There's last year's dry stalks and the new spring shoots coming up in the same place.'

Evaline took off her apron, tied it into a pouch, and began to fill it with greens. She gathered tender, grey-green lamb's quarter; flat, shiny clusters of a plant she called greasy bacon; pink-stemmed purslane, even young dandelions and thriving wild mustard.

'How do you know which ones are good to eat?' Wilbur asked. 'You might be picking some that's poison. Lots of stuff is poison. Your own Grandpa Stevens says so.'

'Well, my own Grandma Malone showed me how to pick greens. She says greens don't grow anywhere as well as along the railroad track—flowers, too. Grandma Malone says she gets disgusted sometimes, because the railroad company, without even trying, can raise better flowers than she can.'

'Evaline, you're always talking and bragging about your relatives.'

'I guess you're just jealous because your kinfolks don't live around here, Wilbur.'

'That's nothing to be jealous about; and anyhow, my Aunt Annie lives in Beaumont. That's only ten miles away. Next winter, when Orville goes to high school, he's going to stay with her and help with the chores.'

Perhaps this was as good a time as any to tell Wilbur something she dreaded to mention. 'We might move to a high school town,' she blurted out, 'so Lester can go to high school.'

'A high school town!' Wilbur exclaimed. 'Move away from Middling? I don't believe it. You are not! You wouldn't like it, Evaline.'

'Oh, I might. There'd be sidewalks; and I'd have a doll buggy, and I'd wheel my doll buggy up and down on those sidewalks all day long. I'd have a fine dish doll like your sister, Dorothy, has to wheel around.'

'About one day, and you'd be tired of wheeling that doll buggy and wish you were back in Middling, riding old Tarpaper. You can hardly do anything in a town. You can't help railroading. Why, they wouldn't even let you walk along the track like this.'

'Why not?'

'Too dangerous.'

'What would be so dangerous about it?' Evaline asked.

'Well, nothing,' Wilbur explained, 'but they'd claim there was.'

'Don't town kids know enough to get off the track when they hear a train coming?' Evaline asked. 'Don't they know when the trains are due?'

'No, they're stuck away back on some little dinky street.'

'Doesn't anything ever happen in a high school town?' Evaline asked.

'Sure, but nobody much knows about it, except maybe to read about it in the paper a week after it's all over. Things happen, but the town marshal or the Red Cross or the police judge or somebody else takes care of it. Now in Middling, suppose somebody stole some chickens. You'd know who stole them, because you'd see the feathers around and figure out who had a big chicken supper.'

'Yes,' Evaline agreed, 'and your dad and my dad and Mr Clark, and some others would decide what to do—call the sheriff maybe, or tell those chicken thieves to pay for the chickens, or maybe make them move away from Middling.'

'That's right. Everything that happens in Middling happens to almost everybody. But it's not that way in a high school town.'

It sounded dull to Evaline. 'Wilbur, how come you know all about high school towns?'

'I stayed with my Aunt Annie in Beaumont for a whole week. I didn't like it. I feel sorry for Orville.'

'Why does Orville do his reading down at the depot?' Evaline asked.

'Nobody bothers him,' Wilbur answered. 'At home, Dorothy is always whining around, or my mother makes him work. She'd make him do more, except that she thinks he's special because he likes to read and study so much. She thinks he's going to be a missionary.'

'What are you going to be, Wilbur?'

'I'm going to have a mule farm, raise mules, and take them on boats to Spain.'

'When I go to Spain,' Evaline said, lifting her head high, 'I'm not going on a mule boat. I'm going just as good as anybody on a regular steamboat. I'll just walk around on the deck all day and not be bothered about mules.' Evaline marched briskly down the chat to demonstrate.

She was about midway between the depot and the section house when a bright ribbon of green caught her eye beyond the right-of-way fence. 'Look how that watercress has greened up on the stream. I'm going to get some of that, too.'

She climbed the low wire fence and slipped carefully between the two top strands of barbed wire so as not to snag her sweater. Wilbur waited impatiently until her apron dripped from the plants taken from the cold water. After she and Wilbur ran to the section house with the lard, oil, and greens, they went back to the depot with the order hoops.

The freight room was a good place to play even if Orville did refuse to budge from the best coffee sack. Evaline inhaled the grand odour of the freight room. It was the mixed smell of coffee, tobacco, leather, fertiliser, livestock mash, sour cream, and bananas.

She and Wilbur reinforced a natural fortification formed by four fat bags of sugar. Around these they rolled a case of shoes, four snagging spindles of barbed wire, and some wooden boxes of chewing tobacco. Whole coffee beans, dug from a strutted burlap bag, were their only rations; and Wilbur refused to use this as food. He preferred to regard the coffee as chewing tobacco and to risk his life to gain the freight-room door to spit. They stopped playing when they heard a team and wagon coming. Botan Courtois backed his mules up to the freight-room door.

Pushing a wagon straight back to the open door was hard for the mules. Botan cursed them in English, then in French. He popped a great long whip over their backs and abused them in two languages.

'Ho, ho, back, back, you childless devils!' he yelled. 'Sons of Satan know who, haw! Allez-y! Allez-y!' Botan pulled on the leather lines, long and limp as black snakes in the wagon bed. The mules flung up their heads and threshed in the harness. The trace chains rattled at their flanks where the hair was worn off the hide. Their big haunches lowered almost to a squat as they pushed against the wagon. Their hoofs thumped against the timbers placed between the house-track rails for a driveway. The steel of the wagon wheel rims ground against the steel of the rails they crossed.

Mr Bates, wearing a station agent's cap squarely on his head, hurried out of the office with a freight list on a clipboard. He helped Botan load most of Wilbur and Evaline's fort into the wagon. It was bound for a country store at French Creek, which was far off the railroad. Wilbur, glued near the wagon, did not miss a word of the profane insults Botan poured on the straining mules to make them pull the heavy load.

Botan's cries still echoed in her ears when Evaline heard a train whistle. She knew it was time for the fast southern special, and she liked being in the depot when it tore past. The whistle was closer, at the Middling crossing. There was a deceptive lessening of noise. Then all at once, the train was on them. The locomotive, as it passed, cried as if the sound of whistle and bell were torn from it. The depot shook on its foundations. Evaline could see the very rails move up and down as the great black blur of the train passed over the rails. Even above the roar, she knew Wilbur was shouting something. He waved his arms over his head.

In the sudden contrasting quiet that followed the passing of the train, Wilbur yelled on, too far into his pretence to stop. He was cursing a stubborn team using the words of Botan and other teamsters. Then he realised all was quiet except his own voice which died away under Evaline's shocked stare.

'Wilbur Bates! Why, Wilbur Bates!'

Wilbur shrugged and tried to dig more coffee beans from a sack.

'Why, I'd be too proud to talk that way. For little, I'd walk right into the office and tell your dad. Then you'd get the whipping you need and wouldn't have that on your conscience. Say, come to think of it, that's what you do every time a fast train passes, isn't it, Wilbur? It makes such a big racket that you yell cuss words, thinking nobody can hear you.' Evaline shook her head. 'You've got an awful lot on your conscience, Wilbur.'

'It's my conscience, not yours,' Wilbur mumbled. 'And I don't run tattling. I'm not going to do it any more, anyway.'

Another far-off locomotive whistle sounded. Wilbur brightened. 'There's the local.' He looked up the track. 'Yes, sir, it's in the block. Maybe Hotbox Barr will be the conductor today!'

'You just want to talk about something else,' Evaline said. But she too was interested in the coming freight train. Its familiar whistle brought her brother Lester running to the depot. Even Orville came to life, and they were all lined up—Orville, Wilbur, Evaline, Lester, and Mr Bates—like a reception committee when Hotbox Barr swung off the freight caboose.

It seemed to Evaline that everything about Hotbox Barr was the same colour. His wool cap with earflaps tied over the top might have been dark blue at one time. Maybe his shirt had been tan and his trousers grey. But now, everything, even his skin, was a tan-grey mix, not greasy, but well-shined. She noticed his hands when he checked freight bills of lading. His hands were brown and polished like the table in Mrs Bates's sitting-room.

'What else to unload at Middling?' a brakeman asked.

'Five cases of belly wash and a tomcat,' said Hotbox Barr as he shuffled through freight lists.

The children waited to see what the brakeman carried from the car. It turned out to be five wooden cases of soda water and a sewing machine. Hotbox renamed pieces of freight and most of his crew as well. This day it was made up of Little Britches Mallory, Never Sweat of Hoxie, Mud Eye Miller, and Beaner Baumgartner.

The local freight train waited on the side track for everything. It was in no hurry. There was a fast passenger train coming, and Hotbox had orders to wait at Middling. The engineer climbed down from the engine cab and crossed the track to the depot to visit with the rest of the crew.

Hotbox sniffed and began examining the freight room. 'Smells funny in here,' he said. Against the far wall, he found open bags of stock feed. He took a handful of dark mash and held it under his nose. 'What's this unholy mess, Bates?'

'Scientific hog ration, and don't get those bags mixed up,' Mr Bates warned. 'Lester Stevens here has helped me mix it according to the recipe put out by the book farmers.'

'Mr Bates has the best hogs around here,' Lester spoke up. 'They're better than Volwrath hogs, and Volwrath doesn't have to farm and railroad both.'

'And how's the tin-can garden coming?' Hotbox asked as he looked at a row of plants crowded into the light of a small window.

'Iowa did the best without fertilisers,' Lester explained. 'Then Illinois, but Missouri is catching up with a little fertiliser.'

Hotbox shook his head. 'Soil from all over the Union, just to see which will sprout the best corn. Everything's going on in this depot except railroading, Bates.' Hotbox sat on a sack of navy beans with a tan-grey hand on each tan-grey knee. His eyes were popped out at the seriousness of the situation. 'Bates here, cluttering up company property with a lot of hick schemes, and there's always a passel of brats around this depot. Some day the division superintendent is coming around here, Bates, and he'll really clean house.'

'There's nothing in the rule book against it,' Mr Bates said. 'Not in the whole 747 rules. I've——' He did not finish but lunged over Hotbox on the bean sack, knocked over a can of sprouting corn, and pushed Evaline and Wilbur aside to get to the office. Mr Bates had heard the telegraph key sounding code letters that were the Middling call from the train dispatcher.

Evaline jumped when the semaphore on top of the station clanged to the 'stop' position. Mr Bates had pulled a big lever inside the station to change it.

'Stopping No. 24 at Middling! What a way to railroad!' Hotbox seemed disgusted.

One long pullman car after another pulled slowly by the depot. Steam billowed up round the wheels until finally the great, long train came to a slow stop. Pullman passengers looked briefly out of the windows, wondering at the delay. They saw so little at Middling that they turned back to their newspapers, or to each other. Evaline saw the dining car with little tables and white cloths. Waiters set the tables for lunch. She remembered her hunger that wasn't exactly hunger.

'Come on, kids,' said Hotbox. 'She'll be here awhile. Come on board and see a real train.'

The boys followed Hotbox. Evaline longed to go, but there she was in a faded cotton dress, tattered sweater, and shoes worn through at the toes. Mama wouldn't want her to get on a train looking like that. She could only wait for Wilbur to tell her about it.

'Why didn't you come, Evaline?' Wilbur asked later.

'I wasn't dressed fitting,' she answered proudly.

'You should have come and seen everything in that train the way I did,' Wilbur said. 'I saw a woman in there, and do you know, she had her hair chopped off, and her fingernails painted red, and she was smoking like a man.'

'Wilbur Bates, that's a lie, and you know it,' Evaline said fiercely.

'It is not a lie.'

'Yes, it is. You didn't see any such thing. First you cuss. Then you lie. It's too much in one day. I don't know if I want to play with anybody that acts that way.' Evaline jumped down from the high freight-room door and started to run towards home. Wilbur followed her.

'Wait, Evaline! Listen!' He was panting as he caught up with her. 'You can go home if you want to, but, boy! I'm not! After a while, my dad and I are going to set trotlines across the river in that long hole across from your house. You can go with us.'

'No, I'm going home,' she said and ran on. When she looked back at Wilbur, he was drawing something in the chat with a pointed stick. He looked lonely, but it served him right for telling such a whopper. Still, fresh fish would be good, and they might get some on the trotline.

Supper that night was wonderful. Dad filled his plate with dark boiled greens.

'Evaline picked these greens, Joe,' Mama said.

'I could eat a wash pan full,' Dad said.

Out of a jar, Grandpa Stevens fished slices of his precious hot peppers, too fiery for anyone else in the family to eat. He hummed his satisfaction as he ate. Mama had worked hard all day, but now she had time to sit back and watch the old man, so pleased with something different to eat. Then she began to laugh and couldn't stop. And they all laughed, and Grandpa hummed on, and didn't even know what was funny. Then Opal brought in a vinegar pie, so good that Evaline didn't even mind when Dad bragged on Opal for making it.

'Mighty good, Opal,' Dad said. 'A little sharp and just right! It tastes mighty good this time of year before garden truck comes on.'

After Evaline ate supper, all the annoying feeling of being hungry for she-didn't-know-what was gone. She wasn't even mad at Wilbur any more. She wondered if there were any fish on the line. Just as she finished the dishes, she saw Wilbur coming to the section house.

'Evaline,' he called as he pounded on the screen door, 'hurry up! My dad says you can come with us to run our trotline.'

It was getting dark when Evaline came from the river with Mr Bates and Wilbur. There were two big catfish on the line, and Mr Bates gave one of them to Evaline. Then he and Wilbur went down the track towards the depot and the agent's house. Evaline was alone. She started across the second sidetrack towards the section house. Then she saw someone coming with a lantern and knew right away that it was Dad.

'I thought you might need a light,' Dad said. She held up the fish that glistened in the lantern ray. 'Say now, are you still bringing in the grub? Folks can almost live off the land in spring in these parts—the right-of-way, the stream, and the river. There's not many places like this.'

Evaline wondered if he was thinking of a high school town. Dad took Evaline by the hand. 'This little old hand feels like a bird's wing, but it can do a lot more.'

Dad's hand felt big and hard from carrying steel rails and driving steel spikes. Evaline remembered the lucky-day feeling she'd had in the morning. All day she'd been free. Now at dark, her dad had come for her with a lantern. It was an extra-lucky day, she thought, as she watched Dad's long legs scissoring, scissoring the lantern light.

3

IT RAINED ALL day long, a steady hard rain. Evaline was soaked by the time she reached Clark's store, which was crowded with men kept from spring ploughing and planting by the downpour. Evaline stood on the dry-goods side, and Mr Clark did not see her for a long time. She was glad to get the spool of white number 60 thread and start for home and dry clothes.

In the afternoon, there was nothing more interesting to do than play 'Hide-the-Thimble' with Gertrude and Joe Junior.

After supper, Dad took hymn books from the chimney-corner shelf, and they all sat near the lamp and sang. Mama chose 'Let the Lower Lights Be Burning', and led them in such a loud, clear voice that they almost drowned out the beat of the rain on the tin roof. Opal wanted to sing 'In the Garden', which Evaline thought was a silly, slow song. But she sang along anyhow so that she could get her choice, which was 'Onward, Christian Soldiers!'

They sang until bedtime. It was still raining. When Evaline woke the next morning, the windows were rivers of rain. She looked out of the front door across the track to the river.

'Mama,' she asked, 'is there going to be high water?'

'Yes,' Mama answered.

'Do you think it's going to be real high water, Mama?'

'High water, nobody knows how high. When it rains all day, all night, and into the next day, there's always high water; nothing to do but wait and see.'

But Mama didn't wait. She worked. Her sewing machine seemed about to run away with itself. She had two dresses to make for Mrs Whiteside, and this was a good time to get at them.

Opal worked on her embroidered quilt patches and cautioned Evaline not to jump around and cause her to stick her finger.

Out in the kitchen, Lester was making an awful mess shelling seed corn. All winter, as his Grandfather Malone fed cattle on the Ab Whiteside farm where he worked, he put aside the longest, best-filled ears of corn. By spring, there was a big bag of the best corn to be shelled as seed for the new crop. Lester liked anything to do with farming, so he was content.

Gertrude and Joe Junior didn't seem to mind the rain. They wrapped rags around sticks of wood and had about a dozen stick-babies to play with.

Since Evaline was aimless, Mama set her to tacking carpet rags, a job she hated. Tearing rags into inch-wide strips wasn't so bad. Every strip she tore had to be sewn to the end of another strip and wound on a ball. Tacking was tiresome, and the ball didn't seem to grow. She wondered what Wilbur was doing. If she complained about the rain, she knew Mama would say, 'We're in the dry. Think of your dad out on the track, maybe wet through to the skin.'

By noon the river began to spread over the bottom fields. The bank willows became islands of fresh spring green with brown, swift water swirling all around them.

Still it rained. They watched the water creep higher and higher. Evaline went to the back door to let Arnold in out of the wet. She heard a familiar step, firm and deliberate, in the front room and knew Dad was home early. After he put on dry clothes, he sat near the heating stove to get warm. Evaline came back to her work and sighed over a pile of rags.

'What have you been doing all day, Water Skipper?' he asked Evaline, calling her by the nickname he alone used.

'Sewing on these old carpet rags.'

'Have you been sewing on them all day?'

'I guess it's only a day, but it seems like my whole life,' Evaline said. 'I sure hate to sew carpet rags. Whenever it rains, I have to work on them, and I never get done.'

'I'll get rid of them for you,' Dad said. He gathered the cloth strips and stuffed them into the stove.

'Joe! What on earth are you doing?' Mama shouted.

'I'm just helping Water Skip get rid of these carpet rags.'

'Stop it, Joe,' Mama said and tried to take the strips from him. But she got tangled up in the strands and began to laugh.

'No use to stop now,' Dad said, 'is there, Evaline? The ends are all on fire, might as well throw the rest in. Rag carpets are just something to trip over anyhow, nothing but dust catchers.'

Then he began to dance a shuffling jig. When Evaline saw the bottom of the basket which she had never seen empty before, she jumped up and tried to follow Dad's jig. But now he was doing the back step. Next he gave Mama a swing that took her right off her feet.

'Joe, stop all this stamping around,' Mama protested. 'You'll shake the stovepipe down and set the house afire.'

'There's plenty of water to put it out if I do,' Dad reminded her.

'What a time to carry on, with the water coming higher and higher.'

'Might as well. We can't stop the rain.'

Trains pulled slowly through Middling that evening, although the tracks on a high roadbed were still above water. Slanting rain fell across the beam of locomotive headlights which shone out over a sheet of water. All the low ground was flooded. When Evaline went to bed, she noticed that Dad's hip boots and lantern lay by the front door.

She woke in the night and knew that Dad was going out to inspect the track. She heard the lantern chimney come down and set in place. After the front door closed, she heard the squeak of Mama's rocker and knew that her mother was up too.

The next morning was different from any Evaline could remember. She looked out of the window, but there were no railroad tracks. There was only water. The depot was there, but it was surrounded by water. Brown water lapped at the edge of the section house yard. It was still raining harder than ever. Mama seemed to be thinking of something else and would answer no questions.

When they heard a train whistle in odd, short toots, the Stevens children crowded to the window to see how a train could come through such high water.

'Two men are on the front, on the steps of the cow-catcher,' Lester said.

'One looks like Dad,' Opal said.

'It is Dad. What's he doing?' Evaline asked.

The freight train moved like a languid dragon pushing through the swirling water.

'The other man is Hotbox Barr,' Evaline said. 'They have long poles pushed out in front of the engine.'

Mama looked over their heads. 'They're feeling with poles to see if the track is still there.' Mama shook her head. 'Dad's been out nearly all night. I've never seen the water so high, and it's still rising.'

Evaline watched the green of their ground inch away under the water that was creeping up the road. The children watched the track side, then the road side of their house.

'There's a rowboat!' exclaimed Gertrude. 'It's coming right up the railroad track.'

'A boat on the track! A boat on the track!' Joe Junior shouted.

'It's Orville and Wilbur Bates in Mr Clark's high-water boat,' Evaline said.

Orville rowed easily over the rails. Wilbur stood up in the boat shouting something to them.

'Who does he think he is,' Opal snorted, 'boss of the Middling flood? He'd better sit down in the boat.'

'They sure look funny out there in all that water, in that little boat—like boys that lived away off somewhere else, in Holland maybe; like somebody there'd be a story about in a school reader. I wonder if they feel that way,' Evaline mused.

'Orville knows how to row better than I thought he could,' Lester said. 'I'll bet their dad sent them to see how high the water is on that boxcar set out on the sidetrack. It's almost over the car wheels.'

'I wonder what's in that car?' Evaline asked without expecting an answer.

An hour later they saw the boat again, and this time Dad was in it, rowing hard right up to the front porch.

'Get ready to leave the house,' were his first words when he came, dripping wet, up on to the porch. 'It's still coming up.'

Evaline helped Opal and Lester carry canned food from the flooded cellar up to the attic. Her legs ached from hurrying up and down steps. Clothing and bedding had to be carried up too. Dad, Mama, and Lester put dressers and chairs on top of tables, but there didn't seem to be any way to move everything above the reach of threatening water. Evaline and Gertrude remembered the hens; they put sweaters over their heads, jumped across the chicken yard puddles, and opened the door of the shed so the hens could fly off to the hillside.

When Evaline came in from the soggy island that was the chicken yard, she stopped a moment to hear what Mama said.

'How's the track, Joe?' Mama asked.

'Can't tell anything about it. There isn't much high

water south of here. Do you know, Mr Bates is still down in that depot? He and the telegraph operator were there all night, reporting to the train dispatcher. When the water came in the depot, he just put on his hip boots and kept on at that telegraph key. Then it got over his boots, so he climbed up on the telegraph table. That's where he was, last I saw of him, sitting up there cross-legged on the table, drumming away on the telegraph key, and papers floating all over the office. Tickets got wet in the ticket case, so he put them on the table to dry; but the water came on up, and they floated out of the window. Freight is bobbing around in the freight room.'

'What will he do if it keeps rising?' Mama asked.

'Climb out on the roof, I guess,' Dad said. 'It wouldn't surprise me to see Mr Bates up on that depot roof, telegraphing the dispatcher that railroading is still tricky at Middling.'

By noon, water crept under the front door of the section house and darkened the wood floor. Dad took Opal, Lester, Gertrude, and Joe Junior in the boat across the flooded yard and road. Gertrude and Joe Junior looked small and fearful, huddled together on the boat seat. Gertrude held Arnold and tried to straighten his matted wet fur.

Joe Junior's wave made Evaline feel forsaken. She wished she were in the boat too, going towards the high hillside far from the water that swept over everything. The other children started to walk over the ridge to Grandpa Malone's. She could hardly wait to go too. She wanted to leave the section house where things had

become strange and unfamiliar, but she must wait for the second boat.

Dad rowed back right up to the porch post. Evaline jumped into the bobbing boat. They waited for Mama.

'Nora, Nora,' Dad called. 'Come on. What's keeping you?'

Mama stood two inches in water when she came to the front door.

'It's Grandpa, Joe. He says he won't leave.'

'What?'

'No, I can't get him to budge. He says the world is not going to be destroyed by flood. It will be by fire next time, he says, and he's not going to leave his home because of a flood.'

Dad groaned. 'Can you beat that for a contrary old man?'

He got out of the boat and sloshed into the dark house. Evaline rocked along in the boat for a while, then followed Dad. The boat was tied to the porch.

Grandpa Stevens sat in his favourite chair and did not seem to notice the water around him.

'Now, you're coming,' Dad shouted, 'if I have to carry you out like a baby.'

'No, I'll stay here,' Grandpa Stevens said. 'The rest of you go. Flee the wrath, but I'll not leave.'

'Hard-headed old——' Dad began, but Mama put her arms round Grandpa and began to talk to him as if he were Joe Junior.

'Why, Grandpa, we can't go off and leave you here alone. Why, we couldn't do that a-tall. We're all going over to my folks, over to Malone's, and it will be

43

kind of like a reunion, and they are all expecting us. Like as not, my mother will make a spice cake, the kind you like, and you wouldn't want to miss that.'

'Miz Malone makes the best spice cake I ever ate,' Grandpa Stevens declared. 'But I'm not going over there today. It's too bad a day. I'm going to stay here, daughter, but you go. I'll be here when you come back.'

Evaline thought of Grandpa Stevens alone in the house which would be dark as a pocket. She thought of the water coming up and up. A terrible sick feeling started in her stomach, rose up and set her heart pounding. Maybe Opal and Lester would run off and leave Gertrude and Joe Junior. Perhaps Gertrude would be scared and wish she, Evaline, were with her. Evaline began to cry. Everything was so wet. There was no place to wipe her eyes.

'Now don't you cry, Evaline,' Dad shouted. 'We've got enough water around here without your tears.'

But Evaline didn't even try to stop crying. She was so tired, and the thought of leaving Grandpa Stevens alone in the flooded house made her sob and sob.

'Nora, you and Evaline follow the others,' Dad said with a sigh. 'I'll stay here with him.'

'If you stay, I stay,' Mama said.

'No use risking us all just for Pa's whim,' Dad said. 'Get in the boat. I'll take you to high ground. Then I'll come back.'

"Twon't be by flood,' Grandpa Stevens called after them as Dad pulled the boat again into the muddy water.

Evaline watched Dad row back to the section house, which was like a yellow houseboat in a wide, swift, brown river. Pieces of driftwood were piling against one end of the house. Why, her dad was the best dad in the whole world, and he was going back into that big flood. Evaline felt wretched even before she realised that Mama was crying, and Mama hardly ever stopped to cry.

Everything was still the same, yet different. She looked at things standing in water—the stockpen, the cottonwood tree, the boxcar on the track. Then she noticed a dark, wet band above the water on the boxcar. There was a similar dark mark on the trunk of the cottonwood tree.

'It's going down! It's going down, Mama!'

'It is! It is!' Mama agreed.

Dad had seen it too. He waved and smiled.

'They'll be all right now, Evaline,' Mama said.

4

THE NEXT DAY the Stevens children raced back towards Middling along the ridge path. Each wanted to be first to view the flooded valley. Evaline led. No one could outrun her.

The marvellous drying sun shone everywhere. The ridge path threaded through post oaks with sun-spotted trunks. Blue jays called from the branches just coming into leaf. Evaline jumped and ran over the ground soft with old leaves and thick moss still sodden from rain. The path became more distinct as it led into the school-yard on top of the hill above the railroad.

Like a great sheet of silver, the river flashed in the sun. Evaline had never seen anything so beautiful. A lake would not be so wonderful, for it would not have the powerful current of the moving stream. The section house, depot, railroad tracks, were all above water now, and the dreadful threat of being swept away was gone. It was all familiar again, there in the sunshine, with just enough water in the road to make things interesting.

Quiet water lay backed up in the lowest part of the road near Clark's store and the depot; and here, Wilbur Bates went willingly by boat on all sorts of errands. He took Evaline in the boat to Clark's store and agreed to let her help in his ferrying service.

'My dad's depot is a fright,' Wilbur said. 'When

the water went down, it left two inches of mud, and all
the papers got wet. Even my dad's station hat floated
away. Let's go see what he wants us to do now.'
Wilbur kept the boat in the flooded road opposite the
depot, and called across: 'What now, Dad?'

'Bring the mailbags over from the post office.' Mr
Bates stood, clipboard in hand, at the edge of the muddy
backwater.

'Say, you really missed it, Evaline,' Wilbur said as he
rowed, 'by running off to your Grandpa Malone's.
You just missed the best flood we ever had in Middling.'

'I saw enough of it. It didn't seem much fun yesterday. I like this part better.'

The high water went down a little each day, but
farmers still kept from work crowded the stores and
talked of how high the water had come up on various
landmarks. It was a record flood, all right, and Mr Clark
put a high-water mark on the side of his store to show
future generations.

He also announced an auction, for the merchandise
in the flooded boxcar was intended for his store. It was
damaged by water and would be sold to the highest
bidders. Everyone looked forward to the auction.

The flood was over, all except the talk. Only Joe
Stevens was still concerned. He told his family that the
roadbed was weak in spots from the water. 'No wash-
outs, but it will take watching,' he said. 'The high banks
above the track are loose and spongy.'

'Good old sunshine will take care of that,' Evaline's
mother said. 'I want to get a garden in soon now.'

Maybe Dad listened in his sleep, for he was the only

one to hear the roar in the night. It was tense, low questions that woke Evaline.

Mama asked, 'What is it, Joe? What are you doing up so early? Turn the flashlight on the clock. It's only four in the morning, still pitch dark.'

'Something woke me up, Nora, a roaring sound. Get a light. Help me find my shoes and the lantern. Something's wrong.'

Opal and Gertrude woke too. From a south window, Evaline and Opal watched the bobbing light grow smaller as Dad walked down the track away from the depot and the section house. Opal yawned and went back to bed, but Evaline kept watch. After a while, Mama asked, 'Do you see anything, Evaline?'

'I think I see a little, tiny light. Yes! I do, Mama. It's Dad's lantern, and the way it's moving around, he's running.'

Mama put a coat over her nightgown. Evaline felt under her bed for her shoes. Despite her sweater, Evaline's teeth chattered from the early morning cold and from excitement.

'What is it, Joe?' Mama called.

'It's a landslide! On the track! Milepost 68, at the curve. Run to the depot, Nora. Tell Lorenz to stop Number 85. I'll set torpedoes and try to flag it, in case you can't get to the depot in time.' Dad rushed to the toolhouse where the warning torpedoes were stored.

Mama could run, but not as fast as Evaline. 'Remember, tell him, south of Middling, Milepost 68,' Mama called after her as Evaline flew ahead.

Evaline thought of the long passenger train coming

fast, of the curve that hid the blocked track. The train would be derailed by the landslide if the engineer didn't get warning. Running in the dark was like running in a dream. Hard as she tried, something seemed to pull her back and keep her from reaching the station. She knew where the switch marker was beside the rail, so she took a great leap over it. She fell on the loose ballast. Her knee burned as if a piece of chat were stuck in it, but she ran on towards the yellow lamplight showing in the depot window.

Bud Lorenz, the night telegraph operator, kept himself awake during his long shift by playing checkers with another operator fifty miles away. By telegraph, they informed each other of moves and kept identical boards. The station north of Middling reported Number 85 had gone by. The whistle blew for Middling, and Bud Lorenz thought he'd just have time to break his opponent's king row, before interrupting the game to report the fast train's passing to the dispatcher.

A breathless little girl with hair falling into her wild eyes burst into the telegraph office. Words seemed to choke her before she could speak them.

'My dad says to tell you there's a landslide on the track,' Evaline pointed south. 'Post 68, by the curve——'

The operator leapt up; checkers flew. He reached for the levers at the end of the telegraph table. Evaline flattened herself against the wall to keep from being knocked down. A chain rattled, and the semaphore high over the depot clanged into the red 'stop' position.

The headlight of Number 85 shone. The engineer

whistled for the crossing a few yards from the depot. He was not expecting a stop signal at Middling. The train came on at full speed, its whistle moaning across the countryside.

There were three jarring sounds, deep yet sharp. Those were the torpedo caps Dad had set on the rail to explode from the weight of the engine. Could the engineer feel the jar and hear the boom over the wail of the steam whistle and the clang of the bell? There was a wonderful hissing sound as the air brakes went on. The cars that had been flying by the depot slowed. The click as the cars crossed the rail joints dragged to a slower beat as the train passed the depot. From the window, Evaline and Bud Lorenz watched the red signal light on the rear coach move slower and slower until it came to a full stop.

Bud Lorenz turned back to his keys and, with a shaking hand, began the dot-dash code to inform the train dispatcher of a blocked main line at Middling.

Evaline slipped out of the depot, and there was Mama coming towards her with a flashlight. Mama grabbed her and almost hugged the breath out of her. 'Evaline, well I declare, Evaline, why you just beat any white-tailed deer I ever saw. M-m-m, how you did run! That chat just flew and I couldn't keep up with you. I stood out here and tried to help flag with this flashlight.' Mama laughed and seemed about to cry a little too and hugged Evaline terribly tight again. 'Well, say now, we're going to get a good early start on our work today. It will soon be daylight, and here we'll be, Evaline, out on the railroad track in our gown tails.'

They laughed as two girls would and hurried home to the section house.

But the day was too exciting for work. All the Stevens family went to see the landslide as did everyone else in the countryside who heard of it. Passengers got off the train, milled around, and looked at the obstruction that had almost derailed them. The engineer told, over and over again, how he was warned almost simultaneously by the depot signal, torpedoes, and two flag lights. He knew the danger was great and had just time to stop the train.

The landslide was a huge mass of earth, stones, and trees that slid down, leaving a great raw scar on the steep hillside above the track. The single track was buried under tons of debris. A work train was coming, but it would take many hours to clear the track. Evaline held Joe Junior by one hand and Gertrude by the other, taking them with her wherever she went. She heard snatches of talk about 'backing her out'. She knew the plan was to return the passengers to St Louis rather than delay them at Middling until the landslide was dug from the track.

Evaline saw everyone—Grandpa and Grandma Malone, Ab and Mrs Whiteside—everyone but Wilbur. She didn't dare ask Mr Bates where Wilbur was, because the Middling agent was the busiest man on the railroad next to the train dispatcher. Finally she saw Orville with Lester and some older boys and asked him.

Orville shrugged. 'Oh, he's gone off on old Tarpaper on some crazy idea of his. He was here a while ago, and then he got a fool notion about being cut off from civilisation and made out he had to ride out for supplies and a lot of tommyrot.'

The passengers, reconciled to a delayed journey, were ready for a backward trip to Beaumont where there was a roundhouse that could turn the engine. The conductor was getting the dispatcher's final orders from Mr Bates when Old Tarpaper loped around the bend by Clark's store. At first, Evaline didn't see Wilbur, who was lying low as a jockey on the horse's neck.

'That a runaway?' the conductor asked.

'No, it's my boy, and he knows better than to ride an old horse that way. I'll tend to him as soon as I get you started.'

Mud spattered from Tarpaper's flying hoofs. As he passed Evaline, she could hear an 'Ump-ump' sound as if his insides were jarred from a long run.

'Stop, Dad, wait!' yelled Wilbur from the road. 'There's a 'nother.' Wilbur's blue eyes were popped out, and his red hair looked wilder than usual. He tried to talk but his words went in the wrong direction. He swallowed them instead of spitting them out.

''Nother what?' Mr Bates imitated.

'Up there.' Wilbur pointed north. 'Bigger than the other one.'

'Other what, Wilbur?'

'Landslide!' Wilbur finally gasped.

'How far? Where?' the conductor asked.

Mr Bates was already headed for the telegraph table.

Wilbur told Evaline all about it as they rode at a much slower pace to the horse lot behind the Bates house, to release old Tarpaper.

'I just thought I'd scout along the ridge,' Wilbur said, 'in case there were any looters hanging around, fixing to rob the passengers or do any looting. There's nearly always a lot of looting you know, Evaline. I figured the lay of the land. I thought if I was a looter I'd sneak along the ridge, and while everybody was up looking at the landslide, I'd just sneak in and loot the train, baggage car and mail car and everything. So Tarpaper and I were just skirting along the ridge above the track. All at once, Tarpaper nearly fell down the bluff. A whole raft of rock and dirt and brush and everything had slid right down on the track. So I said to Tarpaper, "Stretch out, old boy, we've got a sand-wiched train".'

'That's what we've got, all right,' Evaline agreed, 'right here in Middling. My dad's section men had orders to help clear the first landslide or they'd have found it.'

In the afternoon when Evaline came home from viewing Wilbur's landslide, she was surprised to see Mr Bates and the conductor of the stranded train hurry-ing away from the section house. 'We'll do the best we can,' she heard Mama call after them.

'About what, Mama? What do we have to do? What were Mr Bates and the conductor doing at our house?' Evaline was a bundle of questions.

'About feeding those folks on the train.'

'Why don't they eat in the dining car?' Opal asked.

'They ate everything in the diner. It only had enough supplies for breakfast.'

'Why don't they go over to the stores and get some baloney and cheese and stuff?'

'At noon they ate all the baloney and cheese both stores had. I guess they ate just about everything in sight,' Mama explained. 'Mr Bates wants us to dress some chickens and stew up a big pot, and Mrs Bates is going to do what she can, and different ones he can get to help. Then we'll serve those folks in the dining car, or make shift somehow. If they had a good supper, it'd put them all in better sorts.

'There's only one thing. We could dress chickens and we could stew chickens, but could we catch them?' Mama put her hand on Evaline's thin shoulder and looked straight into her eyes.

'It would have been easy if we had known and left them shut up in the chicken house,' Evaline said. 'But just look out there! Even the chicken yard gate is open, and the chickens are all over the place; some up on the hillside.'

'I'll get a washtub ready to shove them under when you catch them, Evaline,' Opal said. 'If you can't run down a chicken, it'll be the first thing you couldn't catch. You're always bragging about how you can run.'

'Chick, chick, chickee!' Mama's voice rang out and brought chickens from everywhere. Some, with loud squawks, flew from the hillside right across the road and down into the chicken yard. Mama scattered corn, and she and Evaline stood quietly until the chickens were contentedly pecking away. With a sudden dart, Evaline grabbed two hens at once. They squawked and flapped their wings, but Evaline held them until Opal got them by the legs and popped them under the washtub.

The feeding flock scattered, and it was some time before any hens returned despite the lure of tempting corn. Evaline caught one more. Then no matter how coaxingly Mama called, the chickens wouldn't come close for corn. They walked along the fence poking their heads forward, trying to find a hole big enough to crawl through. Evaline followed stealthily after one hen, cornered her and caught her just as she flew up, beating Evaline's face with her wings.

Chickens were everywhere; and so was Evaline, after them. She lost track of how many she caught. The hens were getting tired of running and would have been easier to capture, but Evaline was tired too.

Finally she heard Mama's voice above the squawks of the chickens. 'That's enough, Evaline. You've done a good job.'

Evaline stopped and closed her eyes. All she could see was feathers.

The rest of the afternoon, the kitchen was a steamy, hurried place. Evaline gladly ducked out now and then to study the stranded passengers, who strolled up and down the track. She was especially intrigued by a young woman who smiled at her.

'Want to come sit on our porch for a while?' Evaline asked.

'Why, thanks,' the woman said. She sat in a porch rocker, and Evaline was shocked to see that the woman's stockings were rolled below her knees and that she couldn't cover them with her short skirt. With a sigh, the stranger took off the hat that had been pulled down like a bucket over her eyes. Her hair was bobbed right off and was an odd red colour like one of Mr Bates's Duroc hogs. But that was not all. When the woman worked with the catch of her purse, Evaline saw that her fingernails were painted red. From the purse she took a cigarette and matches and began to smoke like a man. Evaline tried not to stare and thought of her injustice to Wilbur Bates.

Supper heartened everyone. All the passengers felt better after the meal and the news that their train would be freed by midnight.

Mama came home from serving with four dollars in her big black pocketbook. 'I'm going to leave one in here to spend at the auction,' she said, 'and the rest goes in this mustard jar. That's our cow fund.'

'Or our moving fund,' Dad reminded her.

5

EVALINE LISTENED AS Lester explained earnestly to Mama and Dad his plan to earn money during the summer. Grandpa Malone had agreed to set the big incubator and Lester would raise the hatching of chicks up to frying size. For supplying feed, his grandparents and Ab and Jennie Whiteside would receive a share of the fryers. The rest were for the Stevens family and for Lester to sell.

'I could sell fryers to the train crews,' Lester said. 'They'd take just about all we had to spare.'

'They're always on the lookout for young chickens,' Dad agreed.

'And I thought maybe—just maybe, if I could start saving up, I could get enough to pay some board in town to go to high school.'

'There's no harm in trying, Lester,' Mama sighed, 'but board's awful steady. It comes round every week.'

'Well, maybe not for this year's schooling, but just to get a start,' Lester said vaguely.

A week later the Stevens children, and Wilbur and Orville, started through the woods to Malone's where the incubator had been set.

Evaline loved to run along the ridge path from the section house to her grandparents' home. The trail wound through woods, over creeks, across meadows belonging to Ab and Jennie Whiteside, who owned the biggest farm in the county. Ab Whiteside had many farm hands to help him, but Grandpa Malone had worked for him the longest, was the most skilled and lived in the big log tenant house.

In spring so much happened so fast along the path that Evaline couldn't keep up with it. She wanted spring to wait and give her more time to look. Maple trees were almost as red with new blossoms and tiny leaves as they had been with old leaves in the fall. Oaks were poky with tiny leaves, soft as Arnold's ears. Hickory buds swelled and swelled inside cases of pale green as shiny as Dorothy Bates's hair ribbons. Then the buds burst to show the leaves held like stiff fingers.

Blue violets coloured one spot in the meadow while yellow violets glowed in another. Sassafras, persimmon, and pawpaw with dark red blossoms—everything had a special time and way of growing. Near the log tenant house was a stile over the pasture fence. Beside the stile was a redbud tree and a slender dogwood. The redbud dropped its pink pea-like flowers just before the greenish blossoms on the dogwood bleached to the wonderful white that Evaline thought was the prettiest thing of all to see in springtime.

The walk to Malone's was especially good on this spring day, for so many people came along.

'I hope your Grandpa Malone is at the house,' Wilbur said. 'I like to hear him talk.'

'If it hadn't been for Grandpa Malone, Evaline wouldn't have that fancy name of hers,' Lester teased.

'If it hadn't been for the Wright brothers inventing the aeroplane, me and Orville wouldn't have these fancy names of ours; but how did Evaline get hers?' Wilbur asked.

'Grandpa Malone read a book,' Evaline explained, 'a novel, Mama said it was. There was this girl in it named Evaline, and he liked her best. When I was born, he wanted to name me Evaline, so Mama said all right.'

'I don't know why he wanted to hang that fancy name on her. Do you know what Mrs Ricker said when Evaline was first born?' Opal asked. 'Mrs Ricker took one look at the new baby and said, "That baby looks like a little skinned squirrel," and you know, sometimes she still does.'

Evaline was furious at Opal for repeating this comment. She picked up a clod and started to throw it at her. Lester grabbed her arm, and her anger passed as quickly as it came. It was too nice a day to be mad. But she ran on ahead and was first to see the old brown house with a mist of green forming on the great trumpet creeper that twined over the logs to the roof.

In the side yard, Grandma Malone hung out dark-coloured clothes. That meant her washing was almost done, as did the dying fire under the black washpot.

Gertrude ran to Grandma Malone. 'Are you tired after putting out that big wash, Grandma?'

'Bone weary after rubbing them on the board, but praising God for the strength to do it on this day which the Lord has given us.' Grandma Malone flung out her arms as if she would take in the whole county.

'Now, did you come to see the incubator? This is the day to turn the eggs, and Malone himself is up in the loft turning them now.'

'Hurry up,' Gertrude called to the others, 'if you want to help turn eggs.'

The windows of the log house were small, and it was hard to see inside after the bright outside sunlight. They climbed the narrow, enclosed stairs to the loft where a rectangular case stood on high legs under the sloping ceiling.

There was a strong smell of coal oil everywhere. Grandpa Malone knelt before the chick incubator.

'You're in time to play mother hen and help turn the second tray of eggs,' he said. They all peered through the smoky glass at the rows of eggs in the incubator. The coal-oil burner that warmed it flickered on the side of the box.

'They look just like regular eggs. You wouldn't think so much was going on inside them,' Wilbur said.

'A miracle! The very miracle of life!' Grandma Malone declared.

'All life is a miracle to her.' Grandpa Malone winked knowingly at Evaline. The long, narrow incubator door came down when he unfastened two hooks. He slid out the tray of warm eggs. Carefully he turned them, explaining that hens did this regularly with their feet in the nest. Otherwise the chicks would be lopsided, Grandpa Malone insisted.

Everyone was allowed to turn one row of eggs. Then Grandpa Malone replaced the tray and put the thermometer back on top of it. That thermometer must stay at the temperature of a hen's body, or the whole three-week hatching job would be a failure.

They were all glad to get outside again away from the warm loft and coal-oil fumes.

'Next time you come, bring baskets, Lester, to take home your baby chicks, for you'll be in the chicken business,' Grandpa Malone said. 'Lester wants to try to help make the living, but he'll have his troubles. Chickens are contrary. They are almost brainless. They try to commit suicide. They drown themselves in pans of milk. They let rats catch them. They stand out in the rain with their heads up and drown. They get their feet wet and die of pneumonia. They are cannibals, and they perish from cold. Oh, a chicken is the most stupid thing.

'You'll know in a few days,' Grandpa Malone called after them, as they started a race towards home.

A week later they walked the path more sedately and carefully, for they carried the newly-hatched baby chicks for Lester. The chicks dried off to bits of peeping yellow fluff. Mama helped them put the chicks out of the baskets and under the wide metal hood surrounding the coal-oil heater. Mama said peeping baby chicks was a real spring sound. Lester had patched up an old shed for a brooder house.

After a few days, the chicks were let out in their little yard. If a sudden shower came up, Evaline ran out and drove them into the brooder house. She wanted to help Lester. It was as Grandpa Malone had said. They didn't have sense enough to come in out of the rain. Evaline and Lester spent one afternoon forcing stones into small holes near the floor of the brooder house so that rats couldn't reach the chicks at night.

Evaline was fearful that Arnold might catch a chick, so she shut him up in the cellar under the house when she was unable to keep watch over him. When Mama went under there to get some canned fruit, Arnold came out like a black streak and scared her, so that she said a few more times like that and there would be one less cat in the world.

Evaline asked Lester what she should do with Arnold, and he suggested that she trust Arnold and also keep an eye on him. This she did, and Arnold disdained even to notice the chicks.

On finely ground corn, the chicks thrived and lost some of their down for little wing feathers and perky tail feathers. Lester thought it was not so hard to keep them alive as Grandpa Malone contended. Then one morning he went to the brooder house to feed and water them and found six dead in a corner.

'They've smothered,' Dad said when he came to look at them. 'That's too bad, just when they were getting up nice. A bunch of them piled into this corner for some reason. We'll have to watch them tonight to see that they don't do it again.'

They watched the chickens at dusk when they came into the brooder house. Again they piled into the same corner, so that Evaline and Lester were kept busy clearing them out. For more than an hour they worked, pulling them out of that corner. They did not leave the brooder house until the shrill yapping of the chicks died down to a soft, contented singing. Even so, there were two chickens smothered in the corner next morning.

Every evening someone had to be stationed in the

corner of the brooder house until dark. It became a routine job called 'stirring the chickens'.

Wilbur came one evening to help Lester and Evaline.

'Why do they crowd into this corner?' he asked.

'We don't know,' Evaline said. 'Just orneriness, like Grandpa Malone says, I guess.'

'Why don't you get a bamboo fish pole?' Wilbur asked. 'Stand by the door and nudge them out of the corner with it.'

The sun was low as Evaline ran back with the light pole. She drove a few stragglers into the brooder house, then stood with Wilbur and Lester in the doorway ready to stir chickens.

They did not pack into the usual corner. Instead they began to distribute themselves sensibly under the brooder hood.

'Maybe they're getting smarter,' Evaline suggested.

'No, something must be different,' Wilbur insisted.

'Nothing, except we're standing here in front of the door with a fish pole instead of being in that corner, trying to push them out. We're shutting out nearly all the light, standing in the door, so it's hard to see.'

'Shutting out the light! That's it, Evaline!' Wilbur stepped aside, and the last rays of the setting sun fell into the far corner of the brooder house. The young chickens crowded into the corner towards the light and warmth of those final rays. Their heads held high, scores of wide eyes reflected the sun's low rays.

'They hate to give up the sun, that's all,' Lester said. 'But we'll have to move them, or they will go to sleep there and smother each other.'

'Let's hang a gunnysack over the glass in the door and see what happens,' Wilbur said.

They found one on the fence. After it had been over the door a few minutes, they lifted the bottom a little. The corner was clear and stayed that way until dark when Dad came to see what was keeping the children. They showed him what they had discovered.

'Well, now, don't that beat the dickens and Tom Walker!' Dad exclaimed. 'That's what it was, all right, and you figured it out, Wilbur. I thought we'd have to stir chickens all summer until they were big enough to roost. I thought you wouldn't have any to sell, Lester.'

'Me, too, Dad.'

'Nora! Opal! Everybody!' Dad called.

When Mama came she said, 'The place to stir chickens is in the frying pan. Now we'll have plenty to get up to frying size and some for Lester to sell to the trainmen.'

Evaline felt very happy for Lester, and so did Wilbur when he walked home in the dark down the big road.

6

FROM THE SECTION house porch, Evaline watched
thin, white smoke rise from the smokestack of Number
10's engine. Suddenly, the idle puff of the engine
changed to a sharp throb. Evaline jumped. The smoke
blackened and rolled out in a great cloud as Number 10
pulled away from the Middling station. The cars
smelt hot and cindery. After the train passed, Evaline
watched black smoke thin out and drift over the
countryside. It was only ten in the morning, but
already she, Gertrude, and Opal were grateful for the
shade of the porch. Spring had suddenly turned
to summer.

Gertrude cut paper dolls from a mail-order catalogue.

'Gertrude, are you whacking up the new wish book?'
Opal asked in her shrill voice.

'Of course not,' Gertrude answered. 'Even Joe Junior
would know better than that. This is an old one, "Fall-
and-Winter, 1921–22". There's "Spring-and-Summer"
over on that chair.'

Evaline picked up the heavy catalogue and turned to
her favourite display: a page of parasols made in far-
away Japan. She longed for one of these fragile things
constructed of bamboo and oiled rice paper. The one
she wanted cost one dollar and eighty-seven cents.

'Are you looking at those umbrellas again?' Gertrude

asked. 'Why do you want one, Evaline? They don't seem to go with around here. Do you want it because Dad bid on a job at Oak Bluff and we might move to a high school town?'

'She wouldn't have nerve enough to carry one in a high school town like Oak Bluff,' Opal declared.

'Yes, I would, and in Middling too. I don't know why I want it, but I do. And I'm going to figure some way to get it.'

'You'd better figure,' Opal commented. 'Nobody will give you a cent to buy junk like that, not even Lester or anybody.'

Evaline left the porch and wandered across the road to the cliff where Gertrude and Joe Junior built play-houses. At the edge of the worn play area were wild anemone, bloodroot, buckbrush, coarse wire grass, and a colony of may-apples that grew like small green umbrellas. Evaline dug down beside a light green stem to the white fleshy tuber of root. It came up easily from the soft earth.

She ran with it back to the porch. 'I've figured how I'm going to get my Japanese umbrella,' she shouted. 'I'm going to dig may-apple roots and sell them. Medicine companies buy them and grind them up, and they cure people.'

'Cure people of what?' Opal asked.

'Everything, I guess,' Evaline answered quickly.

'How do you know?'

'Well, it says so on the bottles, but that's not what matters to me. All I'm going to do is dig the roots and sell them by the pound to Mr Clark, and he'll sell them to the medicine company. Come with me, Gertrude, and you can have one too.'

'What'll I do about Joe Junior?' asked Gertrude, who felt a responsibility for looking after her baby brother.

'He followed Mama to the garden,' Evaline reminded her. 'You go under the house and get two gunnysacks, and I'll run to the shed for a spade and hoe.'

Gertrude went with a reluctant glance back at her paper dolls.

'We'll go along the track,' Evaline said. 'Everything grows like sixty along the right-of-way.'

They had a few roots in their bags by the time they saw Wilbur Bates ahead of them on the railroad tracks. They called and caught up with him. Evaline urged Wilbur to join them digging roots, even though he didn't want an umbrella.

'I've got other things to do,' he said importantly. 'I've got to find Wonder Ella. Dad told me to look along the right-of-way for her. He sent Orville the other way.'

'How could a big old sow like Wonder Ella get across the cattle guard?' Evaline asked. 'The way those iron blades are slanted down between the rails on both sides of the crossing, I can hardly get across myself.'

'She could pick her way across somehow,' Wilbur said. 'We've got to find her. She's my dad's best Duroc-Jersey sow. He had her fastened up, but she broke out and ran away.'

'Wonder Ella is such a pet. It doesn't seem as if she'd be the *best* sow too,' Gertrude said.

'She is, and she might get hit by a train and killed if

she's on this right-of-way.' Wilbur climbed the ladder at the block signal post, peered around but didn't see hide or red hair of Wonder Ella.

Evaline stopped to dig patches of may-apple. The sun beat down on her and when she bent near the ground, gnats buzzed round her face. Sweat dripped off the end of her nose, for it was uncommonly hot for spring. For all her work, there did not seem to be many roots in the bag. Gertrude had very few. Stems broke from roots and were lost as she tried to dig them. The three walked along the track. The sun rose higher and reflected the flashing rails into their faces.

'Evaline, I don't care if I have a Japanese umbrella or not,' Gertrude announced. 'I want to go home.'

'Home!' exclaimed Evaline as if she had never heard of the place. 'You'll want an umbrella once you see mine, and I won't let you borrow it, Gertrude. Besides, you want to help find Wonder Ella, don't you?'

'Yes, but I'm tired, and I can't dig much with a hoe.'

'Come on a little piece,' Evaline urged, 'up to second hollow.'

Gertrude dragged her feet and her bag. When they reached a steep ravine leading back between the hills that bordered the track, the scene amazed them.

'Is it snowing?' Gertrude asked.

'It looks like it from all those blackberry blossoms,' Wilbur said.

'I didn't know there was such a good patch up here,' Evaline said eagerly. 'Last year we picked in first hollow. But the Rickers found that patch and trampled the vines down. Don't tell anybody about this place.

We'll pick up here when they get ripe. We'll sell some to Hotbox Barr and to Mrs Shank if she comes with the boarding cars. I'll have money to give Mama for the cow.'

'You're talking mighty big for somebody that might move to Oak Bluff,' said Gertrude, who was not encouraged and begged to start home.

'All right, go back, but keep on the lookout for Wonder Ella,' Evaline reminded her.

'If I see her, she won't mind me,' Gertrude said. 'She's so big. She'll think I've come to pet her and won't let me drive her.'

'That's okay,' Wilbur said. 'Keep petting her until we come, and then we'll drive her out. I want to go a little farther up past the river cut.'

The rails popped in the heat. Evaline was glad when Wilbur said there was no use going farther, and they turned back.

The whistle of an oncoming train sent them into the weeds at the side of the track. They crouched down and closed their eyes to keep from being blinded by cinders. The hot blast and the roar of the fast train passed them. Then a sudden rush of air stood their hair on end. Evaline thought of Gertrude, but knew she would not mind being close to a passing fast train. It was a funny thing about Gertrude. Usually she was not afraid of something that could hurt her but rather was fearful of harmless things.

They came again to the hollow, white with black-berry blossoms, and marvelled at it. The Rickers, who lived down the track and didn't do anything they

didn't have to, wouldn't walk far enough to find it, they decided. Then ahead of them they saw Gertrude. Evidently something near the right-of-way fence interested her, for she was moving that way with outstretched hand through the high sweet clover.

'What is it, Gertrude?' Evaline called.

Gertrude shaded her eyes with her hand and turned to them. 'It's Wonder Ella! I've been trying to get close to her and rub her side with a stick, but she keeps running at me and making funny noises.'

'Look out!' Wilbur yelled just as the huge sow charged at the little girl's back. Gertrude ran to the rails. Wonder Ella stood and shook her huge head from side to side.

The 'Wunk, wunk' of the hog was steady and menacing; not at all like her usual contented grunts.

'Maybe she's been bit by a mad dog,' Evaline said in a fearful voice.

'No, that's the noise she makes when she's got baby pigs and thinks somebody is going to bother them,' Wilbur said knowingly. 'Wonder Ella is the best pig you ever saw except when she's got baby pigs; then she's about the meanest.

'Say! I'll bet she's got some hidden up there by the fence. She must have been lying down, nursing them, when we went by here. That's why we didn't see her.'

Wilbur moved cautiously towards Wonder Ella. She lunged at him as she had at Gertrude. 'Well, we can't leave her here on the right-of-way if she's got a litter of little pigs. They'll get killed for sure, and my dad's counting on those pigs. They're worth more than any others because she's a fine sow. You know, pigs take after their mother.'

'Wonder Ella is not acting very fine right now,' Evaline said.

Gertrude, hoping to see baby pigs, circled above the enraged sow, who caught the sound of movement in the tall grass and weeds. With surprising speed considering her bulk, she turned on her small, dainty feet and charged at Gertrude.

'Climb the fence, Gertrude! Climb! Climb!' Evaline screamed.

The wire wobbled under Gertrude's weight. The sow plunged. Her body and head seemed one solid mass. Gertrude just managed to clear her slobbering, open mouth. Wonder Ella patrolled the fence with frightful 'Wunks'.

'Baby pigs! I see little pigs!' Gertrude cried in triumph. 'One is standing up. It's light pink and just about the cutest thing in this world. It's got a circle of a nose, just like a little, fresh-baked cookie.'

'Never mind all that,' Wilbur called. 'How many are there? Can you count them?'

'One, two, four, five, eight, eleven—eleven, I think, Wilbur.'

'Eleven! That's a record for Wonder Ella.'

'Wilbur, we can't drive Wonder Ella and eleven baby pigs down the track and over the cattle guard, especially with her so unreasonable. What are we going to do?' Evaline asked.

Wilbur thought for a second. 'We'll go up where she won't notice us and see if there is a hole in the fence.'

Loose stones rolled under their feet no matter how carefully they crept, crouched down, in the sweet clover. They reached the fence and safety. Farther down, Gertrude swayed on the fence with the snorting sow only inches below.

'Gertrude, you stay there and decoy her while we see if there is a place Wonder Ella might have got in. Evaline, you go up that way, and I'll go this.'

A few minutes later, Wilbur called, 'Here it is.'

Evaline and Wilbur looked at the big hole under the woven wire and knew the gully was washed by the downpour that brought the flood and landslides.

'Now what are we going to do?' Evaline asked.

'The pigs are right over there,' Wilbur pointed. 'I'll grab one pig and duck down into this hole. Wonder Ella will chase me, and while she's doing that, you put the rest of the pigs over the fence. Then they'll be off the right-of-way and in Whiteside's woods. We'll stop up this hole with brush so they can't get back in.'

'What if Wonder Ella catches you?'

'Oh, I can outrun a big sow like Wonder Ella any day,' Wilbur said.

'What if she runs back under the fence when she sees me touching her pigs?'

'You can work fast, Evaline, like greased lightning.'

Wilbur had a squirming pig before Wonder Ella knew it, but the instant she heard the squeals of her baby she was under the fence and after him. Feverishly, Evaline caught wiggling, squeaking little pigs and put them over the fence.

From the corner of her eye, Gertrude saw that Wilbur

outran Wonder Ella until he stumbled and fell over a tree root. Evaline and Gertrude screamed. Wilbur jumped up and ran on before Wonder Ella's slobbering mouth reached him. The girls' screams diverted the sow's attention from Wilbur. She wheeled and with raging grunts hurtled back for Evaline and Gertrude at the fence. As she ran, her big triangular ears flopped up and down over her small, furious eyes.

'Eleven,' Evaline panted as she put the last of the piglets over, and the girls gained the shaky safety of the top of the woven wire.

Since her pigs were all on the woods side of the fence, Wonder Ella was content to join them. The children gave her time to calm down before gathering brush which she let them pile, unmolested, into the gully, since they were some distance from her family.

The bags of roots were still on the right-of-way where they had been left. Evaline was almost too weary to carry them home. As she spread the roots on the hen house roof to dry in the sun, she thought of the Japanese umbrella and knew she wanted it more than ever.

Next day, right at supper time, she bothered Mama and Opal for the scales which were far back in the kitchen cabinet. She had not looked at her roots but thought they must be dry, for the day had been fair and warm. She was anxious to weigh them. Mr Clark paid two cents a pound for dry roots.

When Evaline climbed the little homemade ladder up to the chicken house roof, she could hardly believe her eyes. The fleshy may-apple roots had shrivelled in the hot sun to almost nothing. They were lost in the big paper meal sack she'd brought out to put them in. Although she knew the sad answer, she placed them on the scales, and watched the black pointer settle to the number one, just one pound, only two cents towards the Japanese umbrella.

She sat on the back step with her chin in her hand. All the family gathered outside, for it was a warm evening. Opal noticed the meal bag—looked inside and said, 'Did you all hear how Evaline was going to get rich digging roots? She was going to dig through to Japan for a paper parasol.'

Dad didn't laugh. 'Everything doesn't always work out the way we expect,' he said. 'I thought I had a chance for a job at Oak Bluff, a good high school town, but another fellow who worked for the railroad longer than I have got the place.'

Evaline crowded in beside Dad on the step. She thought maybe she knew how he felt.

'Evaline, Gertrude,' someone called. It was Wilbur carrying a gunnysack that squealed and wiggled. 'Dad said you could have this.'

When he reached the section house, Wilbur opened the bag and gently shook out a little pig. 'It's the runt pig. My dad said you could have it for helping me get Wonder Ella off the right-of-way. She's got too many pigs to feed anyhow. Here's some skim milk for it.'

Mama said the little pig would have to be fed with a bottle for a while, but would soon outgrow it.

'It'll grow all right, even if it is a runt,' Wilbur declared. 'A runt pig from Wonder Ella is better than the best pig from most sows.'

'It's a fine runt pig,' Evaline said admiringly.

'It's a good thing you found that hole under the fence, Wilbur,' Dad said. 'Other stock might have broken through there, and we'd have had some killed on the track.

'That little pig will grow into a good hog. Lester, I think you can find enough scrap lumber around to make it a pen out behind the chicken yard. Don't make a pet out of that pig, Evaline, and don't let Gertrude make a pet of it, because it will have to be our winter's meat.'

'Would it be worth one dollar eighty-seven cents?' Evaline asked.

'Girls that help bring in family meat and help their dad's job, deserve something special. Order those Japanese parasols tomorrow, Nora.'

7

THE DAYS LENGTHENED. It was still daylight when the bedtime fast train went through Middling. The Stevens children dreaded to go into the section house still stifling from the heat of the long summer day. Evaline hung on the porch post and was first of the family to see Lester riding down the road on Ab Whiteside's mule.

As Lester came nearer, Evaline saw that his face was covered with sweat-streaked dust. Round his blue eyes were white lines kept clean by squinting in the hot sun. His chambray shirt was crusted with white rings of salt from sweating all day in the field.

'I'm going to jump in the river to get cooled off and clean enough to sleep,' Lester called to them. 'Evaline, run and get me some soap and a change of clothes. I can't wait to get into that river.'

Evaline ran. She liked to do things for Lester. She was proud of him for working on a farm.

'He's been getting the wheat ready for harvest. That's hot, dusty work,' Dad said as they watched Lester, slumped wearily on the mule, ride over the railroad crossing towards the river.

'So's swinging a big scythe, cutting weeds along the track,' Opal reminded her father.

Evaline looked at Dad as he sat on the porch step with his long, muscular arms resting on his knees. 'I'm used to it,' he replied.

'Could be Lester's working too hard out there at the Whiteside place,' Mama said. 'He's trying to do a man's work.'

'You couldn't keep him out of the wheat harvest if you tried. It's about the biggest thing that happens around a farm,' Dad said.

Evaline thought it was too. She and Wilbur first noticed Whiteside's big wheat field early in the spring. They wondered how anything could be so green with patches of snow still on it. As the days grew longer, the wheat grew taller and heads of grain formed down in the plant joints. Grandpa Malone showed Evaline and Wilbur how to give the stalk a steady pull so that the top joint came loose. The tender end of the section was sweet to chew.

'Just like any other grass,' Grandpa Malone said.

'This big field will make good wheat, won't it, Mr Malone?' Wilbur asked one day when the three of them stood looking at it.

'It might, it might,' Grandpa Malone nodded, 'barring rust, smut, hail, lodging, Hessian fly, chinch bugs, grasshoppers, and stock break-in.'

But none of these dreaded things came, and all during June they watched the grain grow taller. Once Evaline saw the wind blowing through it and tried to tell Mama how it looked. Mama knew and said that if there was anything prettier than gentle wind blowing through headed grain, she didn't know what it was.

The stalks turned from green to green-yellow, to pale yellow, to gold. Then one evening in early July,

Evaline passed the field of ripe grain just at sundown. It was red, as red as Wilbur's hair, she thought.

The crop was cut, bound, and stacked into stooks which dotted the stubble field.

The threshing crew worked in the neighbourhood. Ab Whiteside ordered two boxcars which stood on the house track at Middling ready to be loaded with threshed grain. Everyone prayed for dry weather until after wheat harvest, though Mama's garden and all the corn in the countryside needed rain.

When Grandma Malone came to the section house, she brought no butter. 'Not a grease spot to be spared,' she explained. 'Everything must be saved for the big crew of men that will come to thresh. The butter's all put down in crocks in the springhouse with cold water flowing round to keep it sweet. The "fat of the land" the threshers are to get when they come to Whiteside's.

'Mrs Whiteside is bound to outdo Mrs Volwrath. Last year some said Volwraths set perhaps just a mite better table because Mrs Volwrath planned out seven sweets and seven sours. Mrs Whiteside heard the drift of the talk, and she's brooded about it. There's to be no question about it this year. The Whiteside table is to be the best of the entire township, just as the wheat is to be top grade, a full sixty pounds to the bushel.'

'Ma, if Mrs Whiteside is bound to cook up a storm like that, you'll need more help,' Mama said.

'I'll have Weezie Ricker, she's biddable; and Marguerite De Clue, Botan's neighbour. She'll come this year too. Could we have Opal as we did last year? She's a fine worker.'

'Mama, Mama, couldn't I help, couldn't I, Mama?' Evaline pleaded. 'Lester's helping and Opal, couldn't I, too?'

'But you're such a mite, darlin',' Grandma Malone considered.

'She's quick, though,' Mama said, 'like a worm in hot ashes. She can whack the peel off potatoes, and she can dry dishes as fast as the night special goes through Middling.' Opal sniffed loudly. 'Of course,' Mama added quickly, 'she can't stir up a cake the way Opal can.'

'There will be traipsing to the cellar because Mrs Whiteside has a shelf of things down there saved for the threshing dinner. Maybe Evaline could help.'

'Oh, I'd be proud to come and help,' Evaline said.

Next day Evaline waited at the depot and told Wilbur she was to help with the threshing.

'You're not the only one,' Wilbur said loftily. 'Ab Whiteside told me they needed all the hands they could get and that I should bring Tarpaper out to haul water or whatever is needed. Old Tarpaper is not really a workhorse. He's riding stock, but he's accommodating and will do anything to help out.'

'When will it be?' Evaline wondered.

'You can't tell when the threshers will get to the Whiteside place,' Wilbur said, 'but when they do, dinner better be ready come noon.'

The threshing machine was pulled into Whiteside's at the end of the long summer day. Early the next morning before the heat bore down, Tarpaper pulled the spring wagon out to the farm. Wilbur drove, and

Opal sat beside him on the hard wagon seat. Evaline sat with her thin legs dangling from the end-gate of the wagon. All the roadside weeds and vines were covered with thick dust. Tarpaper kept a slow walk until Wilbur drove under a low-hanging oak branch and gave it a shake. The rustle of leaves put Tarpaper into an awkward trot since horse sense told him Wilbur might have broken a switch.

The throb of the threshing engine carried over the countryside. Evaline hoped she would see more of the threshing than the work in the farm kitchen. Lester was part of the crew. She wanted to see him at work. She had taken only a glimpse of the big machine beyond the barns when Opal gave her a push towards the kitchen.

'Come on, you didn't come here to gawk,' Opal said.

'But don't you even want to see?' Evaline asked. Opal was already in the kitchen where Grandma Malone, Weezie Ricker, and Marguerite De Clue scurried around the big, steamy room.

Mrs Whiteside, seated beside a work table, balanced a pie on her finger tips and fluted the crust with an expert hand. She spoke cheerfully to the girls. No matter what the weather was, Mrs Whiteside wore a high white collar trimmed with crocheted lace and fastened with a gold pin. Today she wore her best lace-trimmed linen apron. Evaline paused for a minute behind her chair to try again to figure out how Mrs Whiteside pinned her hair into three rolls diminishing in size atop her head, so that she looked quite tall. But Grandma

Malone saw her idle and handed her an empty bucket. 'To the well, darlin', and hurry,' she said. 'Keep the range reservoir full.'

All the rest of the morning Evaline hurried—to the well, to the woodpile, to the cellar, to the smokehouse, to the vegetable pit, to the springhouse.

The big range oven was kept hot to bake pies— blackberry and gooseberry; cakes—spice and burnt sugar. Soon the whole room was like a huge oven.

Out in the summer kitchen another wood range glowed to fry the ham, roast the chickens, thicken the rhubarb and raisin sauces, simmer the dried peaches and apples.

Evaline was sent to the garden to pick fresh lettuce and early string beans. The sun was hot in the garden, but a nicer hot than the kitchens.

The cellar was a lovely cool place by contrast. She was told to go there for jars of tomatoes and sweet corn which this year's garden had not yet produced. She found jars of sausage clouded with the fat that preserved them. She bailed tangy kraut from a big crock under the cellar steps. In the cellar gloom, she located the pickle shelf with the five kinds Mrs Whiteside wanted, besides dewberry and elderberry jelly, pear honey, spiced peaches, and watermelon-rind preserves.

When the meat was done, gravy was made—sputtering red-eye gravy from the fried ham, thick milk gravy from the chickens, streaked gravy from the sausage. Evaline had never seen so much food, not even at basket dinners on the last day of school.

She was sent to far parts of the house to gather chairs

for the long harvest table. In the sitting-room, which smelt of Ab Whiteside's cigars, she noticed the lace crocheted by Mrs Whiteside and placed on chair arms, chair backs, stand-tables, and even on the clock shelf.

She went into the hall darkened by the heavy lace curtain over the glass door. If she stood back, she could see, sure enough, the peacock pattern Mrs Whiteside had crocheted in the curtain. Evaline stood nearer the door and held her hand by the small pieces of coloured glass flanking the door. She watched her hand turn in the light from an odd green to a lovely purple.

The cool parlour was even darker than the hall and had still more crocheted lace. The green window shades were pulled down against the hot sun and its fading rays. The carpet was rose-strewn as was the wallpaper.

She went to the organ, opened it, carefully pumped with one foot, touched a key, and a note sang out in the still room.

She could hardly make out the titles of the books behind the glass doors of the case. She read *Missionary Journeys to Greenland*, *Hiawatha*, *Girl of the Limberlost*, and was puzzling over the next title.

'What are you gawking at?' Evaline jumped as Opal came into the dim room. 'Get a move on you, Evaline. You're supposed to do everything in such a ripsnorting hurry. Are you too weak to carry chairs? You'd better not let Mrs Whiteside see you meddle around in her parlour, or she'll never let you help again.'

'I was just looking,' Evaline protested, as she picked up a heavy oak chair and started for the dining-room.

'Ring the dinner bell, Evaline,' Mrs Whiteside called.

'We're ready to take up, and everything will be on by the time the men wash.'

'Don't stop to gawk, just ring it,' Opal said, as Evaline started towards the bell which hung on the smokehouse gable.

Evaline pulled and pulled on the rope and wondered if the men would hear the bell above the noise of the threshing machine engine.

They did, and came in from the field to wash at the long bench outside the kitchen door. They trooped quietly into the big dining-room where the feast was set. Everyone left off joshing and talking except Ab Whiteside. He made a fuss over Wilbur, saying he wanted that Bates boy to sit by him to see if he could eat as well as he worked. Wilbur was a mighty fine worker, Ab Whiteside declared, almost as good a worker as Lester Stevens, who was the best worker for a boy his age Ab Whiteside had ever seen.

Weezie Ricker whispered to Evaline, 'If Ab keeps bragging on Lester like that, he'll just about work himself to death.'

Evaline saw her big brother square his shoulders and smile shyly as the men looked at him in approval.

But Grandpa Malone didn't seem pleased. Evaline heard him say something about a boy not being a man.

The girls waited on table. From the kitchen they carried plates stacked high with fresh light bread and hot biscuits. They served firm prints of butter, and they refilled bowls of mashed potatoes and bowls of hominy topped off with slabs of butter melting into the plump, softened, whole grains of maize.

Weezie Ricker hurried to the kitchen to ask for the vinegar cruet. 'My pop wants some, and we forgot to put any on. He wants a touch more on the lettuce.'

Grandma Malone and Mrs Whiteside exchanged knowing glances as Weezie hurried off with the cruet. 'For one so used to the best, so knowing about flavours and seasoning!' Grandma Malone shook her head.

The girls poured gallons of hot coffee. Then they cleared away and brought in pans of pie and plates of cake for each man to select his favourite.

Evaline thought it was all over in a very short time, considering how long it took to prepare. Still, Mrs Whiteside seemed pleased. One by one, the men came to the kitchen door to give her and Grandma Malone awed and solemn thanks for the meal.

'I don't want you to go away from this farm hungry,' Mrs Whiteside said. 'We'll be out in the shank of the afternoon with something to tide you over until suppertime.'

Grandma Malone sank down in a kitchen chair and with the back of her hand pushed away the dark hair from her sweat-beaded forehead. 'Such an abundance, Mrs Whiteside, such a great abundance, and most of it right from this very land.'

Mrs Whiteside stood straight and proud. 'Right from the seed up, nearly all of it raised right from the seed up. Now fill your plates, girls. There's plenty left.'

When Evaline sat down, she felt as if she had extra bones in her back, but the weary feeling was gone by the time she ate all she could hold.

Grandma Malone piled lemons on the cleared work-table. 'Now when you girls finish the dishes, start squeezing these lemons. We've ice from Beaumont, you know. There's to be cold lemonade and the rest of the cake taken out to the field in mid-afternoon.'

When Wilbur came to haul the big crock of lemonade, Evaline climbed into the spring wagon to hold the jar steady. Here, at last, was her chance to see the threshers at work. Opal stayed to put pots and pans away, but the other girls and even Grandma Malone went out to the threshing machine.

In spite of the deafening noise, the steady work-horses and mules did not shy when they pulled up close with wagons stacked high with bundled grain. Men caught the bundles on hayforks and pitched them into the machine separator. From a long pipe atop the machine, a cloud of straw and chaff blew to form a straw-stack already as big as a house.

Near the ground in a much smaller stream ran the grains of wheat. Evaline watched it pour into the white cotton bag held by Ab Whiteside himself.

'Look now at that precious little golden flow,' Grandma Malone said. 'All the months to grow, to watch, to work, for that lovely little stream.'

When the bag filled, Ab Whiteside took a sack needle and heavy thread, and with quick overcast stitches closed the top. He was as neat with a sack needle as his wife was with a crochet hook.

A man carried the full, strutted bag to a waiting wagon that would haul the grain to the railroad car at Middling.

Weezie looked among the crew for her father. When she didn't locate him, she asked where he was.

'He's taken one of his spells, like he so often does after dinner,' a harvester told Weezie. The men who overheard this comment laughed a little.

But Weezie seemed troubled and repeated to Evaline that her pop had one of his spells that 'starts in his stomach and sort of runs into his back'.

Evaline looked for Lester and saw that he was taking his turn at carrying full bags of wheat to the wagon. He knelt beside the bag, settled it on his back and shoulder. As he straightened up and walked off with it, Ab Whiteside said, 'A full bushel and a half of wheat, ninety pounds to the bag.'

'Look at that boy shoulder that ninety pounds,' Evaline heard one of the men say.

Once when Lester came to carry a bag, Ab Whiteside said, 'You've been carrying bags all day, Lester. You'd better get an easier job. Trade off with somebody.'

'Oh, no sir,' Lester said quickly. 'I'm not tired. I'll keep carrying bags with the other men.'

Grandpa Malone's wagon was loaded. He called to Evaline, 'I thought I'd see you out here in the middle of things. Where's Opal?'

'Working back at the house.'

'She's worked a-plenty for one day. We'll stop for her, and I'll give you a ride home on the wheat wagon.'

They climbed up on the load. Evaline lay prone on a firm bag of wheat. The trace chains of the harness jangled. The mules' ears flopped, and Evaline grew drowsy.

Fox, the reddish mule, shied at a piece of paper that blew across the road. The lurching wagon and Grandpa Malone's shouts at the mule roused Evaline. Fox plunged in the harness but could not excite Jack, his team-mate, plodding along beside him. Fox took three extra steps to the side for every steady step Jack took forward.

'Consarned mule, Fox,' Grandpa Malone complained, 'he sees too much, sees everything on the road. When we get back from Middling, he'll be tuckered out from looking. Old Jack could still do a couple more loads.'

'Why?' Evaline asked.

'The difference in mules, I reckon,' Grandpa Malone said. 'Whoa-ho there, Fox.'

At the Middling house track, the wheat bags were opened and emptied into the boxcar. Evaline stuck her bare feet into the pile of smooth polished grain and felt rich to be standing in so much of summer. She put her nose close to the wheat and wondered how anything could still smell of sunshine after being put in a dark boxcar.

Opal found her thus, and pushed her head farther into the wheat. 'Still gawking and putting your nose into everything, I see,' Opal said. 'Come on; we're going home.'

Evaline watched Opal's steady stride up the track towards the section house and wondered how her sister could be so matter-of-fact about the exciting day. She thought of Grandpa Malone's comment about his team, 'Just the difference in mules,' he had said. Maybe it was just the difference in girls, she thought. She jumped down from the grain-car door and ran up the track, determined to beat Opal and be first to tell Mama all about the big dinner.

It was dark when Lester came home. He looked pale and went right to bed without saying much to anyone.

Sometime past midnight a fast freight thundered by the section house, but that was not what woke Evaline. It was Mama's quick voice and Lester's low moans. Evaline got up to investigate.

In a circle of lamplight in the kitchen Mama sat with Lester, white-faced and groaning, beside her. She wrung cloths from steaming hot water and put them on his thigh.

Evaline was shocked to see Lester this way. She thought of him as big and beyond trouble. 'What's the matter, Lester?'

Mama glanced up at Evaline, who stood in the shadows at the end of the cabinet. 'He's strained his leg somehow, and it's causing a rising. It'll be easier soon.'

Lester's eyes looked frightened. Evaline felt worried when she went back to bed and tried to sleep.

By morning, Lester's leg was badly swollen and very painful. Dad was troubled and puzzled. 'I don't know what to make of it. You'll have to show it to Dr Brady at French Creek.'

'But he's such a backwoods doctor, Joe. I haven't got any faith in him,' Mama protested. 'Couldn't Lester go on the train to Beaumont?'

Dad considered. 'It's hard to travel by train with a leg like that. We might as well use what doctoring we've got. It wouldn't hurt to see what Dr Brady thinks of it. Evaline, run and ask Wilbur Bates if Lester can borrow his rig to drive out to French Creek this morning. At least, Dr Brady doesn't charge much.'

'He's not worth much, either,' Mama snapped as she helped get Lester ready to go. 'Town folks get to pick and choose.'

The morning dragged for Evaline even though Mama tried to keep her busy. She listened for the wagon and finally, near noon, heard it coming. Lester held the reins limply in his hands. Tarpaper brought him home. They all hurried out to help Lester.

'Dr Brady lanced my leg in three places.' Lester spoke slowly from colourless lips.

Mama and Opal helped Lester to bed where Mama kept careful watch the rest of the day to see that fresh bleeding did not start. Evaline felt desolate as she tried to help Opal around the house. Lester had worked very hard. It didn't seem right that he should be hurt.

When Dad came home from work, Evaline saw something rare. There were tears in Mama's eyes as she told him about Lester. 'It was an awful lot for a boy to go through all by himself.'

'We're a long way from anything but crude doctoring,' Dad sighed. 'I guess Brady did the best he could.'

Dad talked with Lester as he put fresh dressings of clean sterile rags on the boy's leg. Evaline stood by to run and get anything Dad might want.

'Dr Brady said it was strained and pressure was building up and all he could do was lance it.'

'As you carried those heavy bags all day, did you think you might hurt yourself?' Dad asked.

'The men were all bragging on me, Dad, so I felt fine. I didn't think about anything else.'

'It sounded like music to you, didn't it?'

'Yes. It made me feel big, big as a man like you. I thought how I had finished the eighth grade and was wondering what I'd do, and here I was able to do a man's work. Now I don't know what I am, Dad.' Evaline was amazed when Lester sobbed. 'I don't know if I'm a baby or what, but I know I'm not a man.'

'All you need is a little time to become a man,' Dad said gently. 'By then, you'll know you have to do hard things even when there is no one standing by rooting for you. How did you feel coming home in the wagon?'

'Scared,' Lester said, looking steadily at Dad. 'I was afraid the places would start bleeding again, and I would bleed to death. I wanted you or Mama, and I didn't feel big any more.'

'But you were more a man then, than you were out in the wheat field,' Dad said. 'It was harder to have your leg lanced than to work while everyone praised you. Being a man isn't how much weight you can lift, but how far you can carry your trouble without breaking down, like old Job in the Bible. You've had more than your share of misery today. Try to sleep now.'

Dad and Evaline went to the front porch where Mama sat trying to catch a little evening breeze.

'It'll heal, Nora,' Dad said. He seemed thoughtful for a while. 'A boy has to learn. He has to learn what the wrong things are to do. It's part of the harvest, but a boy like that, like Lester, should have more than an eighth-grade schooling.'

8

EVALINE MISSED WILBUR, who had gone with
Orville to visit their grandparents in Illinois. She was
glad Lester was home while his leg healed slowly. He
told her about lots of things she didn't know. When
Opal tried to instruct her, Evaline wouldn't listen. She
pretended she already knew as much as Opal.

As early as they could get started in the mornings,
Evaline and Lester went to pick blackberries in second
hollow. They walked over the hill and down into the
ravine to throw the Rickers off the trail. The arching
briers now hung black with berries bigger than Evaline's
thumb.

Evaline wore overalls to protect her legs from the
briers, but she almost always forgot the straw hat bought
for her at Clark's store. Mr Clark said it was a mighty
good hat for two bits. Still Evaline didn't wear it
enough to protect herself from the rather odd thing that
happened to her each summer. As the sun grew hotter,
it bleached her hair and tanned her face. As the weeks
went by, her hair grew lighter and lighter, her face
darker.

Opal stayed indoors and helped can the berries Evaline
and Lester picked. Opal's hair stayed a nice honey
colour.

When Evaline and Lester got hot and tired picking
berries, they rested on moss and a litter of acorn cups

and hulls under the oak trees. Then Lester would tell her about all kinds of things—why blackberries liked to grow in second hollow, why there were so many old canes that bore no fruit. He showed her how an acorn sprouted, being fed until it took root by the kernel which split in two to make its first pair of fat leaves.

Even though they didn't hurry, Mama was always pleased with the berries they brought. 'Would you look at that now,' she'd say. 'Another lard bucketful. Evaline, you are the fastest berry picker I know. Big berries are about to roll right off the top. But those little hands of yours are getting more brown and scratched every day.'

If Grandma Malone brought cream, Evaline saved all her share to pour over sugared blackberries. Besides tasting good, they looked wonderful when she crushed the berries with her spoon and watched the purple juice swirl into the golden cream. She didn't eat the berries until she crushed and stirred them and the cream to beautiful, pale lavender.

Mama and Opal canned berries and made blackberry jelly and jam until Mama said they couldn't spare any more jars for berries.

Evaline liked early morning best in summer. It seemed extra nice before the sun came down to make everything ordinary. One morning she was up by the time Number 27, the early train she seldom saw, stopped at Middling. She came out on the porch to wave at the train and to smell the early morning. Grandpa Stevens was already there.

' "Joy cometh in the morning", ' he said.

'It says that in the Bible, doesn't it, Grandpa? But you'll be all tuckered out and in bed again by noon. You get up so early.'

' "Joy cometh in the morning", ' he repeated and gazed down the track towards the depot.

Evaline looked too. Joy, indeed, for there on the second sidetrack, nicely spotted near the big cottonwood tree, was something that delighted her.

'Boarding cars! Mrs Shank's boarding cars!' Evaline shouted. She jumped off the porch, dashed through the gate, and ran on stone-toughened feet along the chat towards the string of four cars.

The first looked like an ordinary passenger car except that it was old-fashioned and painted an emerald green. Coupled to it were three dark red cars with small windows placed high and low, seemingly at random.

Evaline swung up the steps of the green car and stood in the open doorway. Inside it was nothing like an ordinary passenger car. At one end was a built-in stove and a sink. Almost the length of the car was a long narrow table where a pleasant-faced woman hummed as she quickly set on plates. She looked up, as if she suddenly felt a presence, and saw Evaline.

'Look who's here!' she called to her husband. 'You should see who is up for all day. It's Evaline Stevens.' Mrs Shank began to sing:

'*My Evalina, sweet Evalina,*
My love for you,
Will never, never die.'

Mr Shank came in from the opposite end of the car and shook hands with Evaline as if she were grown-up.

Mrs Shank continued to make a fuss over Evaline, but did not for a second stop her work of preparing breakfast for twenty men.

'I saw the cars and just came running without asking,' Evaline said. 'How long will you be at Middling?'

'Quite a while this time,' Mr Shank said. 'Our boss, Chris Nelson, has orders to repair the two railroad bridges south of Middling.'

'I'm mighty glad. I'll run home now and tell everybody.'

'Come back after I get the men off to work, and we'll have a visit. I want to hear all the news,' Mrs Shank said.

When Evaline returned to the section house, she found Opal tattling. 'You should have seen Evaline, Mama, streaking down the track with that cotton hair flying, not even combed yet, to bother Mrs Shank when she was trying to get the men fed. She looked like a scarecrow.'

'It sounds as if you'll have plenty of time to visit Mrs Shank,' Mama said, 'if they are going to do so much work at Middling.'

After breakfast dishes were washed and put away, beds made, kitchen brushed out, front room picked up, Evaline watched for a chance to slip away to the boarding cars.

As she ran down the track, she could hear Mrs Shank singing about a dead girl named Hallie over whose grave the mockingbird sang. She sang the lively tune gaily, as if she felt no more sorrow for poor Hallie than the mockingbird felt.

Mrs Shank made beds in the bunk car where the workmen slept. Evaline was a help to her there, for she could squeeze in at the foot of the bunks, climb up on the lowers, and tuck in the bedding of the uppers.

'Now we'll go to my house,' Mrs Shank said and led the way to another car. Half of this car was the quarters of Chris Nelson, boss of the bridge gang. In the other half, Mr and Mrs Shank lived. Evaline was fascinated by this room. It was narrow and compact. The bed, chairs, dresser, shelves, and ornaments were all fastened to the floor or the wall, so that they wouldn't slide around and get broken when a freight engine coupled on to the cars and moved them to another town and another job.

Evaline noticed a little figurine glued to Mrs Shank's dresser and went closer to examine it. The figure of a girl wearing a bathing suit was made of plaster. The mouth was a round 'O' as if the girl was shocked to be seen in the bathing suit even though it came down to her pink knees.

'One of the men gave her to me,' Mrs Shank explained. 'He won her at a carnival and didn't have anyone else to give her to. He's a new man on the gang, Evaline. We call him Lawyer, because he talks so well. I feel sorry for him because he's lonely, not used to living in the cars. He should get himself a wife.'

'How could Lawyer be lonely boarding with all the others?' Evaline asked.

'It's possible even in the middle of a gang. Mr Shank found that out. He worked on this bridge gang, away from home all the time. There I was at home, lonesome; so when Chris Nelson wanted a cook for the gang, I took the job. We've lived like gypsies ever since.'

'Do you ever stop at high school towns?' Evaline asked.

'High school towns, all kinds of towns.'

'Are there jobs for section men in high school towns?'

'Now and then a job comes up for bid on the section. A man with seniority bumps some poor fellow out of his place.'

They went on to the kitchen end of the dining car. It was exactly as Evaline remembered. At the sink was the same square of meshed metal rings used to scour pots.

'Now, what have you been doing all summer?' Mrs Shank asked.

Evaline told her about the harvest dinner and about the secret berry patch where she and Lester had picked more berries than Mama needed.

'Could you pick some for us? Chris Nelson has the contract to feed the men, you know, and he likes for me to put things up in season. It's a saving for him. When I make jelly, he comes putting his nose in the kettle.' Mrs Shank lifted a pot lid, peered in and imitated a man's low gruff voice, ' "Mrs Shank, not so much sugar. Make it thin." '

'We'd like to sell berries,' Evaline said eagerly. 'We've got a cow fund, and we'd put all the money into it. We're figuring on a cow.'

'It's needed with a growing family,' Mrs Shank agreed.

99

Evaline was telling Mrs Shank about the spring flood when she saw Weezie Ricker, Opal, and Marguerite De Clue coming up the track towards the cars. She was disappointed, for now she wouldn't have a chance to tell anything else. They would begin to tell Mrs Shank of who got married and who wanted to get married around Middling. They would start talk of things Mrs Shank felt Evaline should not hear. She'd suggest that Evaline go out and water the chickens. Since she knew what was coming, Evaline said, 'I'll go water the chickens if you still have them.'

'Oh yes, same old place, in the coop under the car,' Mrs Shank said.

There was more incentive to pick berries after Mrs Shank came, and Evaline and Lester agreed to put the thirty cents they received for each gallon into the cow fund. The mustard jar grew heavier.

Evaline was surprised when Mama announced that she was going to take some of the money to buy clothes for a train trip to St Louis.

'But, Mama, I thought that money was all to be for a cow,' Evaline said.

'I've studied about it considerable,' Mama said, 'and I figure there is a time and place for everything, and this is the time for us to make the trip we've talked about so long. Mrs Bates is going to take Dorothy and go to St Louis early on Number 27 and meet Orville and Wilbur in Union Station. They're coming home from visiting her folks in Illinois. She said, "Why don't you bring your children and come along, and we'll all go out to the zoo for the day and come home on the evening train. You don't ever use your railroad pass," she said. So I just said, "All right, we'll go," and there, I'd said it, so there's nothing to do now but get ready.'

'St Louis, St Louis,' Gertrude and Joe Junior chanted as they made a train out of straight-backed chairs.

'I don't want it to be said,' Mama went on, 'that we lived right here in Middling only sixty-seven miles, mind you, from a big city, and you children never were taken there to see anything. And when we go, we'll look like something, be dressed decently, not like a bunch of shiftless.'

'What clothes will we need?' Evaline asked.

'A hat for you for one thing.'

'I could have taken my Japanese umbrella, but Joe Junior put his fist through it,' Evaline said. 'Couldn't I wear the straw hat we got at Clark's? It's like new.'

Opal groaned. 'You see there, Mama. She doesn't know anything about what you're supposed to wear. People don't wear country store hats on a train.'

'Why would I need a hat on the train? It won't be out in the sun,' Evaline reminded Mama.

'Sun's got nothing to do with a hat you wear on a train,' Mama explained. 'It just shows you've got a little pride and that you know you're supposed to wear one, and that you're not just riffraff.'

'The conductor won't let you on the train unless you've got a hat,' Gertrude declared solemnly, and Mama didn't even correct her.

'We're going to have nice patent leather shoes, too,' Mama said. 'You girls will have some like Dorothy

Bates has, with straps round the ankle and little flat bows in front. You've all got to wear your old shoes, what's left of them, until the day we go.'

'Shoes! In summer?' Evaline asked in amazement.

'Yes, so you can wear your new ones when the time comes to go to St Louis. If you don't, somebody will get a stubbed toe or a stone bruise or a cut foot and not be able to wear the new shoes. Then we'll all have to stay home. We'll go to Beaumont one afternoon this week and get the hats and shoes, and I'll take time to make Opal and Gertrude dresses and even a shirt for Joe Junior off that high-water percale.'

'But they will be just like Evaline's,' Opal protested.

'That can't be helped,' Mama said.

'We'll be like those old Scottish families, a long time ago,' Lester pointed out. 'The whole kit and caboodle— everybody—wore the same kind of plaid.'

'I'm getting tired of that piece of goods,' Opal said. 'You've even made curtains out of it.'

'Truth of the matter is, I'm getting tired of it too,' Mama admitted. 'But we've got to make it do the best we can. With nice hats and shoes, the dresses won't be noticeable.'

Evaline thought of the possible cost of hats and shoes and of the many berries required to replenish the cow fund, when a dreadful idea struck her.

'Mama, I don't want to go to St Louis,' she said.

'Why not?'

'Because if we're gone all day long the Rickers will hunt and hunt and find our good berry patch sure as the world. They'd do it now but they're ashamed to, with us right here watching them. Weezie Ricker knows we're selling berries to the boarding cars, and she's hinted she'd like to sell some too.'

'Old Ricker'd use them to make wine if they picked any,' Mama said. 'Anyhow, Evaline, that's something we can't fret over. This is the time to go to St Louis.'

Mama stuck to her plans. They wore their hot out-grown shoes. She took them to a Beaumont store where hats were more beautiful than any pictured in the mail-order catalogues. Evaline admired a white one of fine smooth straw. The brim was wide and there was a soft, black velvet ribbon round the crown. The loveliest part, though, was the blue feather that curled along one side.

'That's genuine ostrich,' the clerk said, as Evaline gently touched the feather.

Evaline stared at herself in the mirror. Then she took off the hat to make sure she'd heard Mama correctly.

'What?' Evaline asked blankly.

'I said if that's the hat you want, that's the one we'll get.' Mama spoke just as if feather-trimmed hats were bought every day or so.

At home, Evaline tried her hat on frequently and admired herself in the fogged glass of the dresser mirror. It covered her sun-bleached hair. The wide brim made her tanned face look dark and mysterious. That blue feather was the prettiest thing she'd ever seen on a human head. She stood sideways, looked over her shoulder at herself, and smiled. Opal caught her in this pose.

'You're going to wear out the rest of that looking-glass, Evaline,' Opal taunted. 'I never thought you'd primp from morning until night. You'd think that was the only hat ever was. I've got a new hat too, but I know it's not so great.'

To Evaline, hers did seem the world's grandest hat, and she could hardly wait until trip day.

She didn't feel like herself on the depot platform at Middling where she had stood hundreds of times and watched the oncoming steam locomotive. Now she would not stare at the passengers and wave at them as the train moved. She was a passenger herself in shiny new shoes and a hat to hold on against the rush of air from the train. She was going on beyond Beaumont through towns she'd heard Mr Bates speak to on the train dispatcher's phone.

Aboard the train, Mama sat beside Mrs Bates with Gertrude and Dorothy across from them. Opal and Lester shared a seat. Joe Junior was happy to be with Evaline.

As soon as they were settled, the conductor came to Mama's seat. Evaline was terribly proud of the friendly way he greeted Mama and Mrs Bates. She thought it showed everyone nearby that they were railroad people too. The conductor moved on to Evaline's seat. He stopped and peered under her hat. 'Why, it's Evaline! Say, I didn't know you in that hat, Evaline.'

She looked at the conductor in the blue serge suit trimmed with brass buttons. He wore a flat hat like Mr Bates's station cap. On the front was a metal plate reading, 'Conductor'.

Evaline grinned. 'I didn't know you either, not in

that hat.' Hotbox Barr laughed and moved on through the car. He took passenger runs sometimes, although he preferred his local freight train.

Joe Junior knew that Evaline could not slip away from him. She had nothing to do but answer his questions, point out interesting things to him, and take him to the water cooler for innumerable drinks from paper cups.

A man with a basket balanced on his fat middle started through the car calling, 'Candy, gum, apples.'

Evaline warned Joe Junior to ask for nothing. Mama had told her once, coming from Beaumont, that the little glass lanterns and pistols which the news and refreshment vendor sold for a quarter contained only two cents worth of candy. The polished apples were at least a nickel each. It was a scandalous market at which to buy anything. All the same, she and Joe Junior both looked very carefully at the candy-filled glass lanterns while the basket moved slowly, slowly past their seat.

Their train took siding. Joe Junior hid his eyes against Evaline when the fast train passed as a clicking blur beside them. Then he watched up the track as the fast train grew smaller and smaller in the distance.

'Evaline, what happens to the people when the train gets so little?'

Evaline thought of going to Mama's seat to tell her Joe Junior's joke, for Mama was in good humour, ready to laugh at anything. But then, Evaline supposed, Opal would criticise her for traipsing around the train, so she kept to her seat for the rest of the trip.

The whole car darkened when they puffed into the vast train shed of the city station. Evaline knew the brakeman and let him help her down the car steps even though she didn't really need any help. She was used to car steps from visiting Mrs Shank's kitchen.

Mama held Gertrude and Joe Junior by the hand. Lester carried the lunch basket, and they hurried along with the rest of the crowd towards the huge station.

The train gate opened into a midway that was a confusion of people, luggage carts, sales booths, and calls about trains arriving and departing. Cries of taxi drivers, shouting the service of their cabs, echoed up to the high-vaulted ceiling of the long midway. Evaline understood only a few of the calls. Mrs Bates steered them through all the noise to a place with marble floors and a sweeping staircase.

People lined up before windows to buy railroad tickets. At one end of the great room, they heard dishes rattling, and saw people eating there in a lunchroom. Families sat on benches, read, and napped. There were little stands that sold newspapers, cigars, jewellery, and dolls dressed like Indians.

Gertrude turned her eyes upward to the high ribbed ceiling. 'First time ever I knew St Louis had a roof over it.'

Mama heard Gertrude and began to laugh, just an ordinary laugh at first; but then, she began to whoop between 'Ha-ha's' and to run out of breath. 'Please, Mama,' Opal begged, 'don't get one of your laughing spells right here in Union Station. Everybody will be looking at us.'

But Mama couldn't stop. She had a day to enjoy

herself, and Gertrude had said something that struck her as funny.

'I guess we're in for it,' Lester said, and they all waited until Mama had strength enough to walk on.

'We'll go to the upstairs waiting room,' Mrs Bates said. 'I told Orville and Wilbur to wait up there. Their train is already in.'

Evaline's new shoes made a fine click on the marble staircase. Mama was almost to the top step when she said, 'I declare, Mrs Bates, if I didn't know I was in the middle of St Louis, I'd think I heard guinea fowl.'

'It's a scandal the way you can't understand those train callers,' Mrs Bates said.

'But I never heard one make a noise like that.' It appeared for a moment that Mama might start laughing all over again.

'There's Orville,' Lester announced, 'over by that post, reading, you might know.'

They all rushed over to Orville, who seemed embarrassed at seeing the people he knew best in the world.

'Where's Wilbur?' Mrs Bates asked.

The guinea cry rang through the waiting room. Orville looked grim.

'Wilbur's down at the other end of the waiting room. I wouldn't sit with him, not even on the train, because of those things he's bringing home. They yelled on the train too.'

'What things?' Mrs Bates asked.

'A pair of guineas.'

They found Wilbur in an isolated alcove of the big waiting room. On his lap he held a cardboard box cut with irregular air holes that indicated animal life inside. When high, piercing cries came from the box, Wilbur shook it gently and tried to look unconcerned.

'Grandma said I could have them if I could catch them,' Wilbur explained.

'We can't carry those squawking things round the zoo all day,' Mrs Bates said. 'It would upset all the animals. We'll take the box to the checkroom.'

They checked the guinea fowl, whose cries mingled with the shouts of train callers, taxi drivers, and news vendors.

There was a long, exciting streetcar ride through the city streets, now shimmering with heat, to the zoo.

As they walked along looking at the animals in cages, in ponds, and in pits, Wilbur told Evaline about his trip from home—of the spirited horses he'd ridden, big fish he'd caught, and deep pools in which he'd swum.

Evaline saw animals whose existence she had doubted. In the tiger house, she was amazed at how much the big dozing Bengal tiger resembled Arnold. It lay in the same position when it slept. Surely, it would not be fierce but as docile as Arnold, if petted. Then she had another thought.

'Say, Wilbur, if Arnold was as big as that tiger, do you think he'd eat me the way that tiger would?'

'Well I should say so. That's a cat for you. I like horses better,' Wilbur said. 'Let's get out of this hot building and go see monkey island.'

At noon, Mama and Mrs Bates located picnic tables in a shady grove and unpacked the baskets of cold fried chicken, homemade light bread, ripe tomatoes, and boxes of big sugar cookies. Then Mama opened her pocketbook and gave everybody a nickel to buy soda water at the stand. Evaline got her favourite strawberry, and Wilbur had lemon.

After lunch, they followed more shaded paths past the bear pits, the seals' pool, and the elks' pasture. They stopped to rest on some benches.

'Where's Joe Junior?' Mama asked.

He didn't seem to be anywhere.

'I thought he was with you, Evaline. Didn't you have him by the hand?'

'I did a while ago, Mama. But he just let go while I was looking at the hippo. I thought he was with you or Opal or Gertrude or somebody.'

'Lester, go back the way we came, past the bear pits, and look for him,' Mama said in an even enough voice. 'I'll stay here by these benches in case he comes here. Opal, you go back to the lion house.'

Lion house! Evaline thought fearfully of the great beasts she'd seen there.

'He was crazy about monkey island, remember?' Wilbur asked. 'I'll bet he went back there. Come on, Evaline, we'll look.'

Evaline was nearly crying. She knew she should have taken better care of Joe Junior. Gertrude could have done better.

'Don't worry,' Wilbur said reassuringly, 'kids are always getting lost in the city, and they always get found. We'll probably find him first, at monkey island.'

He wasn't there. Evaline's worry grew as they

hurried back to the benches to see if anyone had found him.

He had not been found. Mama and Mrs Bates conferred on what to do next when a friendly-looking man came up the walk leading Joe Junior.

'Looking for somebody?' the man asked.

Mama told the stranger how terribly much obliged they were to him.

'I saw him wandering round alone, looking so hard he didn't know he was lost, and I remembered seeing you folks up this way.' The man glanced at the girls' dresses, then at Joe Junior's shirt. 'I figured he was one of the clan,' he said as he walked away.

'Clan! That's it, Mama, like those old Scottish families I was telling you about,' Lester said.

Mama laughed and hugged Joe Junior. 'It wouldn't do to lose the least one of the clan.'

Of all the things they saw, Evaline liked the bird cage best. It was as big as Ab Whiteside's barn, and inside were beautiful birds of all sizes, proud of their fine feathers.

'I wish that peacock would spread his tail,' Mrs Bates said. 'That's a sight for you.'

The peacock pecked corn from the cage floor. His tail was out of commission. Evaline looked back over her shoulder as they left the cage and walked up a steep sidewalk. Then she saw it. The peacock spread his tail!

The sunlight glistened on the blue and green of the glorious tail. Evaline kept her eyes on the growing half circle as she ran so as not to miss a second of the spread. She didn't see the crack in the sidewalk, caught her toe under the rough place, came down hard on her nose, and slid.

Her nose smarted terribly, but it didn't bleed. Mama took a look at it and wiggled it from side to side.

'It's not broken, but you did get a bad skin burn, Evaline.'

'What a place to get it!' Opal exclaimed. 'Right on your nose.'

Evaline tried to forget about it, but it kept burning. She touched it with the tip of her little finger. It felt wet. After a while, it didn't hurt quite so much. Perhaps it would dry right up, and that would be the last of it.

But Opal walked beside her when they came to the camels' lot and said in a low voice, 'You look a fright, Evaline. That skinned place all over your nose is scabbing over and looks worse all the time.'

'I didn't fall on purpose.'

'You could have looked out where you were going and not been running in your new shoes,' Opal reminded her.

Opal walked on to catch up with Orville and Lester. Evaline felt like tripping her, but knew Mama wouldn't understand a thing like that right in the St Louis zoo. Besides, she knew Opal was right. Even the beautiful hat, which she had worn all day, couldn't hide her sore nose.

It felt good to sit down on the wicker seat in the streetcar for the ride back to Union Station. She went with Wilbur to the checkroom for the guineas, which were now mercifully quiet.

Once in the homeward-bound train, things seemed more familiar than they had all day. Joe Junior slept in Mama's arms, and Gertrude slept sitting straight up in her seat. Dorothy Bates mauled her mother's nice white skirt. Evaline and Wilbur put their heads out the window to see the factories and warehouses that lined the track as the train left the city. Suddenly a terrible stench assailed Evaline's nostrils. They had passed a packing plant, Wilbur explained. They saw dwelling houses too, filmed with dirt if they were near factories. Evaline noticed tiny, gritty-looking yards, and the dreaded thought of the unknown high school town came briefly to her mind.

She was relieved when the city thinned out. They began to see farms, fields, and woods. The brakeman called stations. They looked at the depots, much like Middling's, and Wilbur sighed when he saw the agent hurrying along the train platform.

'Seems about a year since I was at Middling and saw my dad. I'm going to get on Tarpaper and ride and ride tomorrow.'

After they passed Beaumont, yellow lamplight began to shine from some windows, for the long summer day was ending. Cooler air drifted into the coach through the open window.

Evaline knew how Wilbur must feel. She was anxious to get home after only a day away. She'd liked going to the zoo, of course, and had many wonderful things to think about. Her nose would heal; she still had her beautiful hat. She was glad, though, to be out of the hot city. She leaned her head just a little farther out the window to feel the cooler air. Her hat blew off and was gone.

'Mama, Mama!' Evaline gasped, as she stumbled back to Mama's seat. 'My hat blew out the window.'

Mama cupped her hands around her eyes and looked out. 'I can just make out the Volwrath barns. We're almost to Middling, so we'll know where to look for your hat.'

'Oh, Mama, I've lost my hat,' Evaline moaned. She was very tired. Her feet hurt from the new shoes. Her nose was terrible-looking, and now she'd lost the prettiest hat she'd ever have.

'Could be Dad will find it when he works tomorrow. That is, if it didn't blow under the train.'

'It would be ruined anyhow,' Evaline sobbed. 'The dew will ruin the straw and frazzle the feather.'

'Might not,' Mama said cheerfully. 'That's a good grade of straw, and the nights are almost hot as the days, so they don't draw much dew. The feather will be all right. Ostriches don't carry umbrellas. You don't want to cry when you get off the train. What will your dad think? He'll think you didn't enjoy your trip to the city.'

'It's no wonder she lost her hat, Mama.' Opal hung over the back of Mama's seat. 'She kept sticking her head out the window. Just look at her, all covered with cinders.'

'Getting full of cinders is part of the trip,' Mama said.

From the train window, Evaline saw Dad standing in the glow of lamplight that shone from the depot on to the station platform. She waved and was first to reach him when they got off the train. The brakeman signalled and swung up on the rear car steps as the train puffed slowly forward, leaving Middling. The engineer whistled for the section-house crossing. The train went faster, faster and soon all they could see of their train were the red signal lights on the rear car.

'The train's gone,' Gertrude sighed, 'and all the people. If they had trouble, like if they were mad at anybody, or sick or anything, seems like all those troubles are gone too.'

'Gertrude, you've been saying daffy things all day,' Opal protested. 'Of course, their troubles aren't gone, just because the train's gone.'

'I just said, "seems like," ' Gertrude reminded her.

For a minute, they were all quiet. They heard another farther-off train whistle, the clang of April's bell, the bark of the Volwrath hound, and the hum of a million insects. Then they all started talking at once, each trying to tell Dad and Mr Bates about the trip.

Next morning Evaline tried not to think of her hat and to avoid the sight of herself in the mirror. She decided to ask Wilbur to go with her to see about the berry patch. The sun beat down on her light hair as she ran barefoot through the deep road dust that was soft as cotton to her bare feet.

She came home very slowly, for Evaline, and explained to Mama, 'We looked along the track for my hat, but we didn't find it. The Rickers found our berry patch, Mama. The whole outfit of them must have been there all day yesterday. The briers are stripped and all tramped down like a bunch of mules had gone through.'

'Well, the Good Lord will ripen more berries,' Mama said. 'There will be more next year. We have plenty canned now, so you don't need to fret over it, Evaline. Don't look so long-faced. You can't stay home and be all the time guarding a berry patch.'

Still Evaline felt wretched, and twice that afternoon Mama had to remind her that when she spoke she was whining and not speaking.

Evaline listlessly set the table for supper when she recognised Dad's step in the front room and glanced up. In one hand he carried his dinner bucket and in the other, swinging it by the velvet streamer, just as if it were nothing, he carried Evaline's hat.

'You found it! Dad found it!' Evaline set down a stack of plates. She examined her hat carefully. 'It's not hurt one little bit.'

She wanted to ask Dad a dozen questions, but she waited until he had eaten part of his supper before she started.

'It's a funny thing about that hat,' Dad said between bites of biscuit, 'we were putting in some new ties along that stretch of track opposite the Volwrath place when along came Clyde Roberts on his motor car, heading for Middling to check the block signals. He's the biggest talker on the Missouri Division, so he stops to chew the rag. Directly, he looks over across the right-of-way fence and says, "Who's that watching you over there behind those high elderberry bushes? A hat is just showing over the top."

'As soon as I saw what Clyde was pointing to, I knew it was Water Skip's hat. So I followed the ditch.

That hat wasn't on the elderberry bushes. They were just hiding a little hollow. That hat was caught on some tall berry briers behind the elderberries, and the whole hollow is just plumb black with dead-ripe black-berries, best patch I've seen in a long time. I didn't notice it because it was blocked off by elderberries.'

After dishes were done, Evaline went out in the back-yard. She felt like herself again.

9

EVALINE WATCHED MAMA guide cloth under the sewing machine's pressure foot up to the stabbing needle. The needle raced, for Mama pumped the treadle fast with both feet. The spool of thread on top of the machine rattled and raised on its holder as it unwound. Sweat stood on Mama's forehead. Above the hum of the machine, she sang, 'Shall We Gather at the River'.

'Mama, that's a baptising song,' Evaline said when Mama stopped the machine.

'Maybe that's why I sing it; makes me think of a nice June Sunday, not this August heat.'

'How can you work when it's so hot, Mama? Don't you get hot?'

'Of course I get hot,' Mama snapped, 'but Mrs Shank wants me to make some dresses for her while she's at Middling. It's just keep at it, I guess. I'm glad I can take in a little money from sewing.'

'Mrs Shank says you're the best one for sewing on the whole railroad division, but I don't even like to pull bastings when it's this hot.'

'Think of your dad out on that hot track. They're putting in ties that have been dipped in creosote to make them last. After handling those ties all day in the heat, the skin is just about took off his hands even through thick gloves.'

Joe Junior was supposed to be taking a nap on a pallet

in the front doorway, but he only dozed and whined from the heat. Not a breath of air stirred in the house. Evaline's cotton dress stuck to her. She knew it was no use to ask Mama if she, Opal, and Lester could go bathing in the river. Mama would say these were dog days, a time of low sluggish water, not fit time for swimming.

Mama finished a long seam. 'If only we'd get a good soaking rain,' she sighed. 'Day after day, not a cloud. The sky's turned over on us like a big copper apple-butter kettle.'

'Tomatoes in your garden are getting littler and littler,' Evaline mentioned.

'I know. I know,' Mama said ruefully. 'It's going to be a burn-out on the garden if we don't get a soaking rain right soon. I was counting on having something put up this year, when Lyle's folks come visiting.'

Suddenly Mama jumped up from the machine so quickly that the light, cane-bottomed chair fell backward. 'I declare, I feel that something is about to befall us. I can't figure out for the life of me what it is.' She grasped her throat. 'I'm nearly choked for a drink.'

'Mama, I'll go to the spring and get a bucket of fresh water. That old cistern water is so warm the chickens don't even like it. Spring water'll be cold.'

Joe Junior sat up on the pallet and whimpered, 'I want to go too.'

'All right, Evaline,' Mama sighed. 'Take Joe Junior with you, but don't carry him home the way you did yesterday. I saw you coming up the road, packing him and the water too. He's too big, and you're too little. It looked like the cat carrying the kitten.'

'Well, he just sat down in the road and bawled,'
Evaline explained. 'Come on, Joe Junior. You heard
what Mama said.'

Evaline and Joe Junior stood at the kitchen door,
dreading to cross the hot stretch of yard to the shaded
road. Across the fence, the chickens had all deserted
their hot, bare lot and sat quietly, with feathers fluffed
and panting beaks open, in the dusty shade under the
hen house.

'What's going to happen?' Joe Junior asked.

'I don't know, but Mama says something.'

At the spring, Joe Junior wanted to wade in the cold
stream, but Evaline forbade him. 'Grandpa Stevens says
sticking your feet in that cold water when you're hot
will give you rheumatism.' Then she considered. 'I
don't know, though, that it would hurt if you put your
face in it.'

She and Joe Junior got down on all fours and put
their faces into the cool water. Evaline opened her eyes,
saw clean gravel, a white watercress root, and a darting
minnow. When she raised her head, she saw a water
skipper skating away on top of the water.

At home, Mama drank two dippers of the fresh water
Evaline and Joe Junior brought. She started to bail a
third when she suddenly announced, 'I know what
it is! Lyle's folks are coming! Why, of course, that's
what it is! They haven't been here all summer. I don't
know why I didn't realise that right away.'

'When, Mama?' Evaline asked.

'Why, almost any time now, I'm looking for Lyle's
folks. It would be as good a time as any. We've got

garden truck in and not burned as yet. The spring chickens are up to good frying size.'

'They think fried chicken is awful good,' Evaline remembered. 'I guess they don't get as much of it as we do.'

Refreshed, Mama went back to the sewing machine. 'I'd better stay with this sewing now, because once Lyle's folks get here, there won't be time for another blessed thing but cooking.' The machine raced faster than ever.

It was settled. Uncle Lyle, who was Dad's brother, was coming with his big family down from St Louis for a visit, just as he came every summer. Opal followed Gertrude and Joe Junior around, fussing at them for leaving playthings lying around. Mama figured where the pallets could be put down on the floor for nine extra cousins.

All the next day, the children gazed down the road every time they heard a car. No one was surprised when a Model T Ford appeared at twilight and slowed down at the section house.

'It's them!' Evaline shouted and jumped up and down. 'It's Uncle Lyle and his tin lizzie.'

It was Lyle's folks all right. All eleven of them climbed out. The children piled out over the doors without opening them. Evaline felt the same odd mixed-up impressions she always felt when she first saw Uncle Lyle. It was like seeing Dad who was not Dad. Their eyes were the same colour and had the same look from them, but Uncle Lyle's hair was dark and bushy with no grey over his ears.

There was Aunt Effie and Rose and Rosetta, Bertha, Alfred, Ferd, Fred, Betty, Bessie, and Avanell. Although they were her own first cousins, Evaline felt shy before this array of kin. Rosetta was Evaline's age. For that reason, Evaline thought of her as her own special cousin. But Rosetta seemed so different from the girl she remembered of a year ago. She was taller and heavier than Evaline. Aunt Effie made them stand back to back and embarrassed Evaline by exclaiming over the difference in size.

None of Lyle's folks seemed shy. They ran everywhere—through the house, around the house, into the chicken yard, up and down the road, over to the playhouse by the bluff. Aunt Effie talked a blue streak to

Mama, pausing now and then to shout, 'Now don't you kids get into anything.'

Gertrude and Joe Junior climbed into the front seat of the Model T. Gertrude pretended to be driver. Joe Junior pushed down hard on a big horn button.

'Ah-ooga, ah-ooga,' went the horn. Uncle Lyle jumped. He was taking tools and tyre patching out from under the back seat.

'I'd better fix this puncture right now,' he said to Dad and Mama. 'We had twelve punctures, an even dozen, between here and St Louis. I had to stop and fix every one. Otherwise, we'd have been here a lot earlier —in time for supper. That's what we were counting on.'

'Oh, now don't you worry, Lyle, better late than never,' Mama said. 'You folks won't go to bed hungry.' She talked and laughed at the same time. It seemed to Evaline that Mama paid a lot more attention to Lyle's folks than she did to her own family.

For all Mama's carefree talk, Evaline knew she was figuring on what to put on the table. She took Evaline aside and whispered, 'Run as fast as you can up to Bates's. Ask Mrs Bates if she can spare us some milk and butter. Tell her not to rob herself, but tell her Lyle's folks have just come.'

Evaline hurried and a few minutes later knocked on the Bates's back screen.

When Mrs Bates came to the door, Evaline announced solemnly, 'Uncle Lyle's folks have come; they've just now come.'

'Lyle's folks! Oh mercy!' Mrs Bates exclaimed,

taking Evaline's bucket. 'Well, I can let you have tonight's milk, and as luck would have it, I churned yesterday so you can have about a pound of butter. I've got another gallon of blinky milk, just going a little sour, but it would make good cottage cheese tomorrow.'

The spool heels of her white slippers clicked across the porch. Once morning work was done, Mrs Bates always dressed as if she were expecting company. Evaline thought it was mighty nice of Mrs Bates to try to help Mama when Uncle Lyle's folks came, just as if they were her kin as well. Then Evaline remembered what Mama told her to say this time and every time she came for milk. She followed Mrs Bates across the porch and into the cave cellar where the milk was kept. 'Mama says, "don't rob yourself." '

Mrs Bates asked, 'How long are they going to stay?'

Evaline shrugged her narrow shoulders.

'Come back tomorrow, and we'll see how much I can spare.'

'Where's Wilbur?' Evaline asked.

'Up in the trees,' Mrs Bates said, 'trying to catch his guineas. He wants them to roost in the chicken house, but they're wild and like the hickory trees better.'

'Please tell him, Mrs Bates, that I can't help him fix the horse lot fence tomorrow, because Uncle Lyle's folks are here. Tell him to come and play with us. Ferd and Fred are asking about him.'

It was almost dark when Evaline reached home. An oil lamp lighted the table where a second supper was set. Mama took the bucket of fresh milk from Evaline and filled the glasses of the children. 'Tomorrow I'll have something better to put on the table for you folks,' Mama explained.

'If there's fried chicken,' Uncle Lyle said, 'I've got this for anybody who'll give me a share.' Uncle Lyle held up a grease-spotted package.

'I'll take it. I'll trade my fried chicken any old day for that store baloney,' Opal shouted and took the package. 'I've had enough of fried chicken to last me awhile.'

Everyone laughed, for Uncle Lyle had traded Opal fried chicken for baloney every summer for a long time.

As soon as Evaline could get a word in edgewise, she told Mama about the blinky milk.

'That's good. I'll put it on the back of the stove now while the fire is dying down. It'll separate a little more. Morning will be soon enough to hang it out to make smearcase.'

Dishes took an awful long time, Evaline thought. As soon as she pitched out the dish water, Mama told her and Opal to help fix beds. They knew their bed must go to Aunt Effie and Uncle Lyle. The bedroom floor was covered with pallets made of folded quilts and comforters for the smaller children.

'You and Rosetta make yourself a pallet with this,' Mama said and loaded Evaline with bedding.

'Where?' Evaline asked.

'Find a place somewhere,' Mama said vaguely.

Evaline went outside to find Rosetta. It was a relief to get out of the stifling house. She found Rosetta among the cousins who ran everywhere, catching lightning bugs.

'How'd you like to sleep outside where it's cool?' she asked Rosetta. 'It's nicer out here than inside. I'll show you a nice place where the grass hasn't all dried up over by the snowball bush.'

Gradually, the section house quieted. Evaline and Rosetta lay on their pallet in the yard.

Rosetta propped her head up on her elbow. 'What's that?'

Evaline listened. 'It's a whippoorwill off in the woods somewhere.'

'I've heard about them in songs,' Rosetta whispered. When a much more shrill cry sounded close by, Rosetta jumped and grabbed Evaline's arm.

Evaline giggled. 'That's only a screech owl. He's over near the bluff by Gertrude's playhouse.'

'It sounds awful scary.'

'Just a little bitty old brown bird,' Evaline explained.

'There's an awful lot of noise for the country,' Rosetta said. 'What is all that chirping?'

'Oh, locusts and bugs and crickets and cicadas and things. The later the summer gets, the more racket there is of a night.'

'It's kind of a nice racket, though,' Rosetta said. 'It's awful on hot nights where we live. We can't sleep. There's no place to go outside like this. The noise is different—babies crying and people quarrelling.'

Evaline jumped up from the pallet and ran off into the darkness.

'I just happened to remember about the chickens,' she explained when she came back and lay down again. 'If you don't fasten the door, they all get out and scatter at daylight. Then I'd have my job of running down a bunch for dinner.'

Evaline wondered why she had felt so shy when Rosetta first came; for now they found lots to talk about. They talked and stifled giggles for a long time; but finally Evaline found herself too drowsy to finish a sentence.

She struggled awake. She was choking. Rosetta's arms were tight round her neck, and a fast night train rushed by. Rosetta held on until the train passed.

'Oh, that nearly scared me to death,' Rosetta gasped. 'I thought that train had jumped the track and was coming right over us.'

They lay back laughing, and the more they tried not to laugh, the funnier everything seemed.

'Mom will be out here with a stick if we don't shut up,' Rosetta said.

They attempted to sober themselves by staring up at the sky where stars seemed surprisingly close to them. Suddenly one streaked across the sky, leaving a long tail of blue light. Then another fell and another. The girls stopped giggling. They were struck with wonder at seeing scores of stars shooting across the heavens. They clung to each other in amazement and a little fear. The universe seemed a vast, marvellous place and they only specks within it.

When they woke next morning, the wonder was gone. Overhead was the same cloudless sky that had blazed down for weeks. They grabbed up their pallet, and in their nightgowns ran giggling into the house to dress.

As she helped Mama with breakfast, Evaline told her

about the stars. Mama nodded. 'Saints' tears. They fall every August. You were lucky to see them.'

They started early to prepare the big noonday meal. Dad dressed the frying chickens. Evaline hung the clabber milk to drip in a flour sack. Mama and Opal baked berry pies. It was getting so hot in the kitchen that Evaline was relieved when Mama reminded her that it was time to get ready for Sunday school.

Rosetta promised to go with her. By the time she was dressed in her good shoes and high-water percale dress, Dad and Uncle Lyle were sitting on the front porch with Grandpa Stevens. The smoke from their cigars drifted into the house. Coloured comic pages of the *Post-Dispatch* lay on the front room floor. Some of the children left the papers to come with Evaline and Rosetta. Evaline didn't really know how many came. Aunt Effie, busy talking to Mama, didn't either.

When they passed Clark's store, all the Sunday loafers on the porch stared and nodded. Evaline was proud to have all Middling know her family had company from St Louis.

The air of the church was stale but cool from being locked up all week. Mrs Bates, who was Evaline's Sunday school teacher, struggled with the big chart to turn over a page for the new lesson. The brightly-coloured picture showed Moses holding up a brass serpent in the wilderness.

In the boys' class, Wilbur Bates looked unnaturally scrubbed; his red hair slicked down with water. But by the time Sunday school was over, his hair had dried with cowlicks standing up as usual.

'I'll come up to your house after dinner,' he promised after Sunday school, and raced ahead of Evaline and Rosetta down the hill.

At home, Mama hurried to serve dinner. Evaline had just time to take off her shoes and put on her play dress before the first table was called for grown-ups and older children. She knew she'd have to wait until second table and eat with the little kids, but she didn't mind since she and Rosetta would be practically in charge.

Uncle Lyle said there was no cooking like country cooking. He thought, honest to goodness, that there wasn't any better eating in the world than fried chicken, sweet corn on the cob, ripe tomatoes, and fresh berry pie.

In the afternoon, Wilbur rode up on Tarpaper. He treated all the cousins to a turn riding. He showed them on which side to mount, how to pull back on the reins, and other points of horsemanship that made Wilbur feel very knowing. Finally Tarpaper, with wet flanks and foamy neck, was allowed to rest and cool off.

The children turned to games. They sat in a big circle and played 'Pleased or Displeased'. They heard a train whistle and stopped to watch a slow freight approach. Wilbur was first to realise it was no ordinary freight. The steam locomotive pulled slatted car after slatted car. The ventilated cars were lined with straw. Above the straw and through the open car doors, the children saw lovely green globes.

'Watermelon train!' Wilbur yelled. 'First watermelon train!'

They saw the brakeman running ahead to throw the switch so that the train could pull on to the sidetrack.

The final sighing of the air brakes was like music to Evaline, for she knew the first melon train of the season was taking siding and stopping at Middling.

With long steps, Dad crossed the tracks and bought four melons from one of the growers who was riding among his melons to market. Dad let Evaline carry a small one on her shoulder to the spring where all the melons were put down in the cold water.

After the watermelon train pulled out, the children started more games. There were enough players for any game anyone could think of. Still Evaline missed Gertrude and Joe Junior and went to ask Mama where they were. Mama was in the kitchen with Aunt Effie starting supper.

'I told Gertrude to look after Joe Junior,' Mama said. 'He was hanging right on to her. They're around somewhere. You folks should come more often, Effie. Gertrude and Joe Junior are so bashful right with their own relations.'

Hunting for Gertrude and Joe Junior reminded Rosetta that they hadn't played 'Hide and Seek', so the game began.

Evaline had used all her good places, gotten in free twice and never been 'it'. She had to think of a new hiding place. Wilbur started for the door that led to the cellar under the house. Evaline followed him.

It was a heavy wooden door, painted yellow like the rest of the section house. The paint was worn away in a semicircle where the iron hook, meant to fasten the door, swung free when the door was opened. A small window at the top of the door was the only light.

Wilbur pushed the door open carefully, so that the iron hook would not clang and give them away. Evaline was right behind him. It took a few seconds to get used to the dim light in the cellar. Then Wilbur backed away and spread his arms to keep Evaline from rushing in. Evaline gasped. On a bench where Mama kept canning jars sat Gertrude and Joe Junior, their eyes big and mute with terror.

On the hardpacked earthen floor of the cellar lay a copperhead snake, big as a bullwhip. Near Gertrude's bare foot a second copperhead was coiled, its head thrust back, tongue darting, ready to strike.

'Don't move, Gertrude,' Wilbur said in a low voice hardly moving his lips. 'Evaline, get a hoe.'

Evaline ran the fastest she ever ran in her life, through the shouting children, to the woodshed. She found the hoe among a tangle of other tools and ran back to the cellar. Gertrude and Joe Junior had not moved. Neither had the coiled copperhead.

Holding the hoe near the end of the handle, Wilbur brought it down hard on the coiled snake nearest the terrified children. As he did so, the second snake near him coiled swiftly and lifted its head. The injured snake was still able to move and crawl towards the rocks of the house foundation. Wilbur struck the coiled snake; then came down hard with the hoe on the injured one in time to keep it from getting away. He struck again and again until both copperheads were killed.

Wilbur panted. Sweat ran down his face. Evaline felt as if she couldn't swallow and hadn't had a drink for a week. Gertrude and Joe Junior sat motionless on the bench, still too scared to move.

Only after Dad took the slain snakes away and carried Gertrude and Joe Junior from the cellar, did Gertrude begin to cry as she tried to answer the flood of questions.

'Joe Junior got tired and whined and said he was hot,' she sobbed, 'and I said, "Well I know a cool place, that's the cellar under the house"; and I took him there, and it was so nice and still and cool under there. He was getting sleepy and so was I; and we were just sitting there; and I saw something on the floor and I could see they were snakes, but I thought maybe they were milk snakes or black snakes that wouldn't hurt us. And I was going to scare them away, and then when I got up close, the light from the window came right in on their mean-looking wide heads, so I knew. I held on to Joe Junior and told him to be still; and we just sat there until Wilbur opened the door.'

'Well, it's over now,' Mama said, holding Gertrude in her arms and rocking her in the big rocker. 'You did the best you could, for a little thing taking care of your baby brother.'

'Wilbur,' Dad said, 'that was quick thinking. I figure you saved Gertrude and Joe Junior from a dangerous poisonous snakebite. I never knew a copperhead to be around our cellar before, and I'm glad you got both of them. Stands to reason, though, they like a cool, quiet place too, just like Gertrude and Joe Junior.'

Gertrude couldn't help but smile a little at having picked the same spot as the snakes on a hot summer day.

'Come on, now. We'll take pot-luck for supper,' Mama said as she put Gertrude off her lap. 'You stay, Wilbur. We'll need you to bring melons from the spring. We'll eat them out in the yard.'

The cold watermelon tasted even better than Evaline remembered from the previous summer. Dad gave her a big wedge with a huge hunk of heart so ripe it broke away from the seeds.

There was plenty of watermelon for everybody. When it was eaten, Mama sent Evaline for a zinc washtub to gather up rinds.

'Give these rinds to the chickens,' Mama said. 'There will be plenty later for me to make preserves.'

When bedtime came, Rosetta and Evaline again put their pallet in the yard, for the house seemed more stifling than ever. They were too tired to do much giggling and talking. Before Evaline fell asleep, she noticed flashes along the western horizon. She knew it was what Dad called heat lightning.

She was awakened by a touch of something on her cheek. It was a drop of rain! A great crash of thunder wakened Rosetta. Rain began to patter around them. They gathered up their pallet, and a flash of lightning lighted their way to the back door.

Inside, the section house was astir. Uncle Lyle was up and kept running to the door to look out as he buttoned his shirt and pulled on his trousers. Aunt Effie and Mama woke the rest of the sleeping children.

'Oh now, Lyle,' Dad said, 'do you think you must leave in the middle of the night this way?'

'It's the best thing to do, or we'll never get that tin

lizzie through that red clay mud,' Uncle Lyle said. 'Load the kids, Effie. Hurry!'

'It's not rained for so long,' Mama said. 'Most of it will soak right in and . . .' The thunder that followed a great flash of lightning drowned Mama's voice.

'No, I know what it's like to be stuck in that long hollow above Middling. There's no bottom to that sticky red clay. We'll get out of here and on to the gravel while the getting is good,' Uncle Lyle said.

The children were excited by the storm and by waking from a sound sleep to start home. In no time at all, the Model T chugged off down the road. The summer visit of Lyle's folks was over.

A heavenly cool breeze wafted through the section house, driving out the heat before it. Evaline settled down in her own bed and listened to the music of the raindrops on the tin roof.

Mama moved through the room picking up pallets. She stopped and sat down on the side of the girls' cot. 'Well, the drought's broken. Lyle's folks have come and gone, and we had a good table to set,' she said.

'And as luck would have it, the first watermelon train came in,' Opal added.

'And Gertrude and Joe Junior were kind of like Moses and the Children of Israel looking on the serpent, weren't they, Mama?' Evaline asked.

'Oh, yes, indeed; well, I should say,' Mama agreed.

10

SUMMER WAS ALMOST over. In the flyspecked window of Clark's store, Evaline saw a poster announcing the Beaumont Fair. She wouldn't be going. That would be too much to expect in a summer that had brought a trip to a big city.

Still she felt a little excitement about the fair. Mama was making three new dresses for Mrs Whiteside to have for fair week. The front room smelt of new goods and was littered with cloth snippets.

One dress was a nice sky blue. Another was pink and yellow checks. Evaline studied the third piece of material. It was an odd pattern of some sort of queer fruit, a little like persimmons, Evaline thought.

Before Mama cut the cloth, she and Mrs Whiteside had looked over the mail-order catalogue and selected the styles to copy.

Mama ran the sewing machine like fury. When she stopped to do some basting, she glanced back over her shoulder at the untidy room. 'Evaline, hurry and pick up this room. Bundle up the scraps and brush out the ravellings. Mrs Whiteside is coming this afternoon to have these dresses fitted. She'll be here any minute.'

In no time at all, Evaline tidied the room, finishing just as Mrs Whiteside drove up in her buggy. The Whitesides had a car, just as Uncle Lyle's folks had, but Mrs Whiteside preferred her buggy for short trips. She said you couldn't beat a buggy for seeing things along the road.

Mrs Whiteside had hitched her horse to the section house fence and started into the house when she remembered something.

'Say, now, I almost forgot. Evaline, run get that box in the back of the buggy, but mind now, don't drop it.'

Evaline lifted the little hatch lid at the back of the buggy. There was a long cardboard box. She thought she'd better peep in so she would know why she must be careful. She lifted the lid and gasped. Gazing steadily upward with beautiful blue eyes were three china-headed dolls.

'Dish dolls,' Evaline breathed, 'dish dolls!'

She carried the box as carefully as if it contained a coal of fire and brought it to Mrs Whiteside, who had been seated in the best rocker in the front room.

When Mrs Whiteside opened the box, Opal and Gertrude and even Mama were amazed.

'Now, girls,' Mrs Whiteside explained, 'I came across these dolls that belonged to my Ethel. A grown woman like her, gone from home, doesn't need them, and she said to me many's the time, "Mom, why don't you give those dolls of mine to some children that could have a little fun with them." So I thought of you girls.'

Mrs Whiteside handed out the dolls. 'And here's something for Joe Junior. We can't leave out the least one,' she said and took from the bottom of the box a tin monkey on a string.

Even though she held it in her arms, Evaline couldn't

believe she owned a dish doll. It was like Christmas at the end of summer.

They thanked Mrs Whiteside and thanked her over and over again.

Evaline took her doll to the light by the front door where she could examine it more closely. It had yellow hair, real hair, Evaline thought, as she touched it lightly. Its face was beautiful, each feature painted carefully and delicately on the china. The eyes looked so real, the cheeks were so pink, the mouth so tiny. The feet and hands were dish too, fastened to a stuffed cloth body. The dress was faded and rumpled. Evaline longed to sew clothes for her doll and wondered if there would be any scraps left from Mrs Whiteside's dresses.

Mama acted oddly though, as if she was uneasy. Her glance darted from Evaline to Gertrude to Opal as they played with the dish dolls. The dust hadn't settled behind the departing Whiteside buggy before Mama said firmly, 'Girls, bring me your dolls. Fine dish dolls like those are not to be played with. They'd be broken in no time. They're to be hung up on the wall and looked at and saved as keepsakes. I'm mighty proud each of my girls has a dish doll. The only dolls I ever had were made of rags. Evaline, run to the woodshed. Get some nails and the hammer. We'll put heavy twine round the dolls and put them up on the wall right now. Move, Evaline.'

'But, Mama, couldn't I play with my dish doll? I'll be so careful. I hardly ever break a cup or anything. I want to make her a dress copied out of the catalogue. I want to learn to sew fast, the way you do, Mama.'

'Go get the hammer.'

'Please, please, Mama! Let me play with her. It won't seem that I have a dish doll unless I play with her.'

'Drop that doll once, and it's done for,' Mama reminded her.

'I won't drop her. After I sew for her, I'll put her away on the high shelf that Joe Junior can't reach.'

'No, Evaline, we're going to hang them on the wall.'

'I'll get the hammer, Mama,' Opal said, 'if Evaline can't do anything but beg.'

Later Evaline watched Joe Junior and Gertrude make the tin monkey climb its cord. She almost wished she had been given a tin toy instead of the too-beautiful doll. At least she could play with it. Gertrude would just as soon play with the monkey as with a fine doll. Opal felt too big for dolls so she didn't mind hanging hers on the wall.

Everybody seemed to have something just his own. Wilbur had Tarpaper. Lester was out at the farm again with all kinds of stock to tend. Gertrude carried scraps to Runt, who had turned out to be her pig. Arnold, who was supposed to be Evaline's cat, didn't seem to belong to anybody. He was off somewhere now, hunting field mice in the tall grass and weeds. Evaline wished she had her dish doll to play with.

The next morning when she woke up, the first thing she saw was her dish doll staring down at her from the wall above her bed. She studied its lovely face. She decided to name it Ethel after its first mistress.

She heard Mama's quick step coming from the

kitchen. 'Girls, get a payday move on,' Mama said briskly as she came into the room. 'I am going out to the Whiteside place today to help your grandma and Mrs Whiteside make apple butter and grape jelly. You can come with me if you want to, Evaline.'

Evaline rubbed a round white scar on her tanned bare foot. It was from a burn she got last year when a spatter of boiling apple butter plopped out of the big kettle on to her bare foot. But that memory was not her reason for wanting to stay home. She didn't want to leave Ethel, her dish doll. Even if she couldn't play with her, she wanted to be able to look at her whenever she liked.

'I'll stay home, Mama, and take care of Joe Junior, and you can light out on the path to the Whiteside place all by yourself.'

Mama laughed. 'Now, how did you know I liked to split out and walk the ridge path of a nice morning like this?'

Mama assigned tasks as she hurried to get ready. 'Gertrude, you make beds and brush out the kitchen and dining-room. Evaline, look after Joe Junior and get dinner for Grandpa Stevens and the rest. Opal, all the sewing on Mrs Whiteside's dresses is done except putting in the hems and pressing. You can fix the hems and see that the pressing is done so that the dresses will be ready for Mrs Whiteside to take back with her this evening. She said she'd drive me home in the buggy, and I suppose after working with fruit all day, I won't feel so much like walking as I do right now.'

Nobody, not even Evaline, could walk the ridge

path to the Whiteside place faster than Mama could. Evaline and Opal watched her start in a run. 'I think Mama is glad to have something new to do of a morning,' Evaline observed.

'So am I,' Opal said. 'I'll start the sewing. You do the dishes, Evaline.'

Evaline knew it was useless to argue that she needed help. It seemed hours before she emptied the dishwater and hung up the damp towel. Then she went into the bedroom to look at Ethel. After a long, long look, she joined Opal, who sewed in the front room.

'Let me put in one of the hems, Opal.'

'Mama didn't say you could,' Opal reminded her.

'Well, she didn't say I couldn't. Please, Opal, let me sew. I can make little stitches. I'm going to sew for Ethel, soon as I get some cloth.'

Opal studied Evaline for a moment. 'You can press if you want to. Make up the range fire and put the flat-irons on and set up the ironing board.'

'Ironing is hot work.'

'You ask to help. When I tell you what to do, you start fussing,' Opal declared.

'Oh, all right,' Evaline said, 'just as soon as I see what Joe Junior's into and tell him to stop it. I'll start the fire.'

While the irons heated, Evaline struggled with the heavy ironing board and set it up firmly. In the chimney-corner shelves back of the hot range, she located the iron stand, the pad of beeswax and the handles to fit on the hot irons. She tested the heat by wetting her finger in her mouth and barely touching the bottom of the iron. A sharp sizzle told her the iron was ready to use.

Opal finished one dress. Evaline smoothed its seams and pressed out the wrinkles. Ironing wasn't such a bad job, Evaline thought, even though she did make dozens of trips between ironing board and stove.

Gertrude and Joe Junior played on the floor under her feet. 'You and Joe Junior better go outside and play, Gertrude,' Evaline warned. 'You're liable to bump over the ironing board, and if you get one of these hot irons on you, you'll know it.'

Gertrude and Joe Junior left Evaline alone in the kitchen. She pressed the second dress and had the fire going when Opal finished the final dress and brought it to the kitchen. Evaline studied the printed cloth.

'Do you think that's a persimmon, Opal?' she asked, 'or is it maybe a pomegranate they talk about in the Bible?'

'I don't know, and I don't care. All I know is, I've done my work. You always want to do everything anybody else can do, so now you do your part and press that dress. It doesn't matter if it has orange pawpaws in it.'

'Evaline! Evaline!' Gertrude called as she burst into the kitchen. 'Listen! Do you hear that? Do you hear it, Opal?'

They listened. 'It's an aeroplane!' Evaline shouted. 'Opal, there's an aeroplane.'

'I can hear,' Opal reminded her and pushed in front of her out of the back door. All three girls ran into the road. They shaded their eyes and gazed skywards, trying to follow the sound of the aeroplane.

'There it is! There it is!' Evaline jumped up and down. 'Over there across the river! It's flying right this way!'

'I see the man. I see the man in it,' Gertrude shrieked.

'Let's run and follow it as long as we can,' Evaline cried and started up the hill path. 'Gertrude, bring Joe Junior. Take him by the hand.'

Wilbur Bates had heard the engine too. He ran to the school ground on top of the hill as he tried to keep the plane in sight as long as possible.

'Where is it?' Evaline called, for she had lost sight of the plane as she ran up the hill.

'Over there,' Wilbur shouted, pointing out the little plane in the bright sky.

Evaline and Wilbur ran along the ridge path, keeping sight of the plane until it became a smaller and smaller speck. Then it disappeared altogether.

Opal, Gertrude, and Joe Junior waited for them to return to the school ground. 'I thought you were going to run clear into the next county,' Opal said.

'That's only the third aeroplane I ever saw,' Evaline panted. 'I wanted to watch it as long as I could.'

'Third!' Opal said scornfully. 'I know I've seen at least half a dozen.'

'There's supposed to be a stunt flyer at the fair next week,' Wilbur remembered. 'I'll bet he came early.'

'You could see the man,' Gertrude said in awe. 'I could see his feet hanging down.'

'That wasn't the pilot's feet,' Wilbur exclaimed. 'That was the landing wheels of the plane.'

'I never did see the man in a plane before,' Evaline said.

Before he turned off for his home, Wilbur admitted that he hadn't either. The Stevens children talked about the plane as they came down the hill path to the section house.

Opal sniffed as she opened the back screen door to the kitchen. 'Smells like something scorched.'

Evaline realised with sickening dismay what she had done. When she ran out to see the plane, she had left the hot iron on the shoulder of the new dress.

Opal lifted the iron. There was a deep brown scorch, the exact shape of the iron. The cloth fell away in the centre, and even the ironing board pad beneath was burnt.

The girls stared at each other. This was too awful to quarrel about.

'Evaline, we've got to make Mrs Whiteside another dress.'

'What out of?' Evaline asked in a hushed voice.

'Goods.'

Evaline grasped Opal fiercely by the arm. 'Opal, we've got enough of that high-water percale left. Mrs Whiteside liked that goods. Grandma Malone said so.'

'Number 10 has just pulled out, so it's after ten o'clock,' Opal said. 'I'll tell Gertrude she's got to get something out of the safe for Grandpa and Joe Junior's dinner. We won't eat. Go up in the loft and get the goods. We'll use this ruined dress for a pattern, whack it out somehow, by guess and by gosh.'

Evaline stumbled down the steep loft steps with the cloth. She and Opal unrolled it and spread it on the floor. Opal pinned on sections of the ruined dress and began to cut. There was just enough material.

Gertrude and Joe Junior came in full of questions; but the grim, silent way their sisters worked soon silenced them. Gertrude was flattered to be entrusted to put cold food out on the table at noon. She promised to take care of Joe Junior, even to telling him stories after dinner.

Evaline's small hands trembled as she ran long basting stitches for the darts of the waist.

'Putting on the collar is the trickiest part,' Opal said. 'I've only done it once, but I've watched Mama do it a hundred times. Keep basting.'

Evaline did not protest. Opal ran the sewing machine, not as fast as Mama did, but not slow either. She rested once, and let Evaline fill the bobbin and run up some long inside seams on the skirt.

'It's more luck than sense that we have some goods Mrs Whiteside might like,' Opal said.

'This dress isn't going to smell very fresh,' Evaline worried. 'There aren't any water rings on the last of the bolt, but it smells musty from the flood water. We won't have time to wash it.'

'We'll do well to get it made by the time that buggy comes up the road.' Opal sniffed the cloth and made a face.

The girls worked on. Grandpa Stevens sat on the front porch and dozed in the shade. Gertrude fell asleep along with Joe Junior. When the machine wasn't

running, the house was so quiet that even the buzz of the flies seemed loud.

Suddenly Evaline said, 'I know what we can do to make it smell good, Opal. You know that cologne and stuff that Grandpa Stevens peddles?'

'Mama and Dad don't want him out on the road alone peddling any more,' Opal said.

'I know they don't, but he wants to go just the same. The company sends him stuff, soap and perfume and that, and he has a box of it hid in the woodshed, so he won't have to send it back to the company.'

'Well?'

'I smelt some of the cologne. It was real nice. We could sprinkle it on the dress when we get done.'

Opal didn't comment. She was on the trying detail of making the sleeves fit the armhole.

The afternoon passenger train pulled into Middling, but the girls didn't take time to look out and see who got on and who got off. They heard Dad's handcar clicking on the rails before Opal turned from the machine and covered the head with its little wooden dome.

'It's done, Evaline, even the hem. Take it and sprinkle some of that cologne on it. I'll build up the fire for supper. That will heat the irons too. I'll press the dress while you set the table.'

Sweet-smelling vapours rose from the dress when Opal pressed it. Dad rested in the front room and waited for supper. 'What's that smell, Evaline?' he asked. 'That don't smell like supper to me.'

Evaline called from the dining-room. 'That's Mrs

Whiteside's dress, Dad.' Dad shrugged as if there was no explanation for the ways of Mrs Whiteside. Evaline hurried, for she knew Dad was hungry. Her back ached from sewing so fast and so steadily. Her hands shook so that she almost dropped a plate. Worst of all, Mama and Mrs Whiteside would show up any minute.

Evaline heard jingling harness and buggy wheels crushing gravel. She ran out to meet the buggy. She wanted to be first to tell what happened, and the sooner the better. As soon as Mama stepped down from the rig, Evaline grabbed her round the waist and pulled her aside.

'Mama, I ruined Mrs Whiteside's dress. I scorched a big hole in it. I ran off to look at an aeroplane and left the hot iron on it. Opal and I made her another one, the same way out of the catalogue, and we used the high-water percale.'

Mama stared at Evaline.

'Anything wrong?' Mrs Whiteside asked. 'Anybody sick or hurt?'

'No.'

'Well, then I guess there's nothing wrong,' Mrs Whiteside commented.

'Could be I owe you for a dress,' Mama explained and repeated Evaline's report.

The three dresses lay on the bed in the front room. Mrs Whiteside nodded over the first two, then inspected the third which was the high-water percale.

'That's the piece I admired at the auction and didn't get.' She looked at the set of the collar and the sleeves. 'I don't see a single, solitary thing wrong with that dress, just as fresh as a daisy. Nora, you got reason to be proud of your girls for turning out a dress like that on short notice.'

'I'll make it right with you if you don't want it for the one Evaline ruined,' Mama offered.

'Oh, I like this one better,' Mrs Whiteside declared. 'I didn't care too much for that other piece. After I bought it in Beaumont and got it home, I wondered why I took it. Keep it, Nora. It'll make aprons or something.'

A great weight of dread lifted from Evaline. She thought Mrs Whiteside must be one of the kindest women in the world. The ache in her back went away like magic. She wanted to run and shout. She ran outside where Opal had gone for more stovewood.

'Oh, Opal,' Evaline shouted, 'aren't you glad? I feel like I could fly, just like that fellow in the aeroplane.'

'No use acting nutty,' Opal commented.

But Evaline did feel like flying. She ran up the hill path and took long leaps down.

After supper they sat on the front porch and sang and sang until they sang the moon up. The bedtime train went through Middling.

'There's something I want you to do before you go to bed, Evaline,' Mama said. 'Go to the shed and get the hammer.'

'What for, Mama?'

'A claw hammer is the best thing to pull out a nail. Take your dish dolls down and pull out the nails. Go ahead and play with the dolls.'

'Mama!' Evaline shouted and ran to Mama's chair.

She tried to hug Mama and Joe Junior both and took care not to get her bare toe under the rocker.

'How come you changed your mind?' Opal asked.

'When I saw how hard you girls tried to make up for Evaline's mistake, today, I got to thinking you could look after a dish doll.'

'Running off to gawk at everything the way Evaline does, she's liable to break her doll first thing,' Opal objected and went into the house to bed.

'It's funny she'd say anything so hateful,' Evaline mused, 'when she worked so hard all day to help me.'

'Don't forget, she helped.'

'I was so glad Mrs Whiteside wasn't mad at me, and Opal didn't seem to care much either way.'

'Remember that, too. Opal's not the easiest book on the shelf. Now run and get the hammer.'

Evaline ran.

II

SCHOOL STARTED, AND there was a new teacher at Middling for the first time in many terms. Still, one thing hadn't changed. School meant shoe leather. The girls wore their patent leather slippers to school since they would be outgrown if saved. Shoes were something you couldn't pass down. At the end of a few weeks, the thin soles wore through.

Evaline showed Dad her slipper. He punched the tissue-thin inner sole with his big thumb. 'I'll half-sole slippers tonight. That will get you kids through until time for laced high-tops. Run down to Clark's, Evaline, and get shoe leather and tacks. You'd better go now while there's plenty of light.'

At the store, Mr Clark put the sheet of brown leather and the box of tacks on the counter and wrote the amount of the purchase on the Stevens' store bill. As he wrote, Evaline noticed some lovely chocolates in the candy case and wondered if there might be some left by the time Dad paid the store bill and Mr Clark bagged up a treat for the family from the candy case.

Evaline put the sheet of leather under her arm, the box of tacks in her sweater pocket, and started home. By the roadside she noticed the giant ragweed far above her head, the buckbrush red with berries, the pawpaw fruit lying on the ground. Everything that is going to get ripe is ripe; and everything that is going to make

seed has made seed, Evaline decided. Wild grapes had
burst on the vine in the warm Indian summer sun, and a
sticky, sweet juice oozed from the bunch Evaline picked.
Cockleburs stuck to her sweater when she stepped to
the side of the road to pick the grapes. Fall was a very
ripe, sticky time of year.

Evaline saw handfuls of corn in the road and knew
the grain had fallen from the wagons hauling corn from
the bottom fields by the river. Wagonloads of pumpkins went by the section house, too. The pumpkins
grew along with the corn and would fatten Ab Whiteside's hogs. By the depot were crates of hens. These
hens, sticking their heads out through the crate slats,
were culled from flocks because they stopped laying
eggs and started shedding their feathers. Evaline remembered Grandpa Malone's remark that, 'The hen
yard looked like somebody had torn up a bedtick.'

Now in the fall, cattle were marketed, too. Steers
from the Volwrath and Whiteside farms were driven
across the right-of-way at the section house and herded
into the stock-pen beside the sidetrack, to await loading
in a stock car and pickup by a cattle train. Evaline and
Wilbur watched the loading of every stock car.

Evaline walked on past the depot. Far off somewhere,
maybe at the Volwrath farm, she heard a sound that
meant autumn to her. It was a wood-saw powered by a
gasoline engine. *Chug*, *chug* went the gasoline engine.
Zing went the saw through a stick of cordwood—*chug*,
chug, *zing*—*chug*, *chug*, *zing*. Evaline ran on the *chugs*
and took a great, long leap on the *zings*. She was at the
height of a long *zing* jump when she saw two men

leaving the railroad track. They climbed the right-of-way fence and started towards the spring, which was ahead of her. She didn't know the men, so she thought they must be hoboes.

Wilbur said fall was a good time for tramps same as for wasps. They looked for a place to winter. One of the men looked as old as Grandpa Stevens. His clothes were a bunch of rags held together in some mysterious way. Over his shoulder was a pitiful pack done up in peeling oilcloth. Evaline knew he was a tramp. He nodded to her in a friendly way. She wasn't sure about the other man, who scowled at her. He was much younger, and his clothing was about as good as anyone's. If he was a tramp, he must be new at it, Evaline thought.

'What you got there?' the old tramp asked, pointing to the brown square under her arm.

'Shoe leather. My dad's going to half-sole my shoes.'

The old tramp nodded. 'That's right. Jack Frost's coming. Gotta have shoes. I've got mine.' He held up a foot, and Evaline was surprised to see not the broken shoes that tramps usually wore, but a fine, new pair of heavy brogans.

'Those are mighty nice,' Evaline agreed. The other man said nothing and did not seem to notice Evaline. He lay down flat on a big stone and sucked water from the spring.

Evaline ran and jumped on as long as she could hear the wood-saw.

After supper, Dad took the shoe-last stand from the chimney corner behind the range. Evaline brought him the different-sized lasts that looked like little iron shoes. He fitted the smallest last on the stand and slipped Joe Junior's little shoe over it. Evaline's shoe took the middle-sized last. Dad tacked on a piece of leather about the size of the shoe sole, then carefully trimmed it with his sharp pocketknife until it was smooth and sole-shaped. Evaline watched him, and picked up the scraps of leather as they fell.

'What are you going to do with those, Water Skip?' he asked.

'I don't know, Dad, but they are nice little pieces of leather. They ought to be good for something, so I guess I'll just save them.'

'You're as savin' as your mom.'

The next morning when Evaline put on her shoes, they felt strange and stiff. But when she went outside, she could not feel the stones beneath her feet. It was a fine bright day. She was glad she had promised Wilbur to go with him to hunt walnuts and hickory nuts. First she must help Mama with Saturday work.

Before the morning work was done, however, the section house was in confusion. Joe Junior had asked and asked where Grandpa Stevens was. Finally all of them—Mama, Opal, Gertrude, Lester, Evaline—realised the truth. They didn't know. No one had seen Grandpa Stevens since breakfast.

Evaline was sent running to Clark's store, to the depot, to the post office. She did not find him. Opal went to the garden to see if Grandpa might be trying to dig carrots. But he wasn't there. Gertrude ran to Runt's pen and called along the bluff by the playhouse. Lester walked towards the river. No one found him.

Mama gathered the children around her. 'Now, did he say anything to any of you about where he was going?' Mama asked.

'He said something funny to me,' Gertrude replied. 'He was going as fast as he could with his cane towards the woodshed, and he said to me, "The old woman has flour on her hair." '

'I'll declare, I've heard him say that many's the time. When Grandma Stevens kept house and they were raising their family, they bought flour by the barrel,' Mama explained. 'When the barrel was almost empty, Grandma Stevens had to lean way in to get any. She'd get flour on her hair, and when Grandpa Stevens saw that, he knew the flour barrel was low and he'd better scrape up some money for another.'

'Why would he say that to Gertrude now when that was a long time ago?' Evaline asked.

'They took to saying that in the family whenever it was time to lay in any kind of stores. I guess he was thinking, it being fall, it was time to get ready for winter,' Mama mused. 'He thought it was up to him to help get in meat and wood. I wonder if he has gone off peddling.'

'He kept his peddling stock hid in the woodshed, in a big box under the chicken-feed sacks,' Evaline said. 'I'll run and see if it's gone.' She darted off and was back in a minute. 'It's gone, Mama,' she panted, 'the extract and salve and cologne and everything, and the pack he carried it in.'

Mama looked worried. 'Your dad doesn't want him out on the road alone. There's getting to be so many cars, and Grandpa goes too far before he thinks to start home. Last time, dark overtook him. Now he's set out again, thinking he can help provide, poor old soul. We'll just have to locate him.'

Evaline found Wilbur at the depot. 'Listen, Wilbur,' she said, 'we can't hunt for walnuts. We have to hunt for Grandpa Stevens. He's gone off a-peddling. He's not supposed to peddle any more. He gets addled.'

'We'd better get Tarpaper,' Wilbur said. 'Hard telling where your grand-dad is, maybe halfway to Beaumont by now.'

Evaline rode behind Wilbur. She liked the squeak of the saddle leather. Leather was mighty substantial stuff. Sometimes Wilbur put Tarpaper into a trot. Then Evaline held to the back of the saddle; but most of the time the horse walked under arches of gold formed by the hickory trees along the road.

Jogging along on the old horse, getting farther and farther away from the section house, Evaline and Wilbur had no way of knowing what was going on there. Dad was hurrying to the section house, although it was only noon.

'Mama,' said Opal, 'here comes Dad. He looks worried. Do you think he knows Grandpa Stevens is gone?'

'Maybe it's something else,' Mama said.

Gertrude ran to tell Dad about Grandpa.

'I've got bad news too—real bad,' Dad said. 'I thought I'd better come and tell you myself before somebody else did and scared the daylight out of you.'

'What is it, Joe?' Mama asked.

'I guess I might as well tell you straight off, first as last. Last night a man was killed. We found him by a campfire on the right-of-way. At first we thought he'd been hit by a train; but then we looked closer and saw he'd been stabbed. He was an old hobo; looked as if he'd been a wanderer all his life.'

'Who could have done away with a poor old fellow like that?' Mama asked.

'That's what we're all wondering. Mr Clark called the sheriff, and he's here in Middling, asking everybody if they saw any tramps last night.'

'Tramps?' Lester asked.

'Yes, there must have been another tramp with him. Maybe they quarrelled about something, and one stabbed the other. This old man didn't have much for anybody to take. He didn't even have any shoes.'

Mama and Dad exchanged that look which Evaline knew but wasn't there to see. It was their way of trying to let each other know something without using words. It was Lester who put into words the question in Mama's mind.

'Do you think whoever killed him is still around Middling?' he asked.

'I don't know, Lester. That's what I came to tell all of you about. He could still be here; but more likely, he hopped a train and is miles down the line. Mr Bates notified the railroad detective. Anyhow, you and the kids best lie low, Nora. Where's Water Skip?'

'Oh, Joe, I sent her out to hunt Grandpa Stevens. Gertrude told you how he went off with his peddling wares. Evaline and Wilbur set out to look.'

'I'd feel easier if you were all here together until we know what happened. It's too bad Pa took it into his head to go off peddling again.'

'He said to me, "The old woman has flour on her hair,"' Gertrude reported. Dad sighed. Then he took his gun from over the front door.

'Is it hunting time already?' Gertrude asked.

'No,' Dad said slowly.

'Let me go with you, Dad,' Lester pleaded.

'You stay here and take care of the family. I'm going with some of the men to look around a little. I won't be gone long.'

They watched him off down the road. It seemed odd

to see Dad carrying a gun before the grey-brown days of the November hunting season.

Evaline and Wilbur rode past the crossroads, past Dr Brady's big, rambling house, past Botan's cabin. They knew everyone they met along the road and asked if Grandpa Stevens had been seen, but there was no word of him.

Wilbur pointed with a limber twig he had broken for a riding switch. 'Right over there in that hollow, behind the gypsy campground is where I found hazel-nuts one year,' he said.

'Why were you way up here hunting nuts?'

'I was really hunting April, our cow. She didn't come home, and I hunted all over the hills for her. I got mixed up; well, almost lost. I found some hazelnuts that day. They're rare. When I came out of the hollow, there I was on the gypsy campground. I could see the road, and believe me, I was glad, too.'

'Did you find April?'

'No, the river was low, and she waded across and got into Volwrath's clover field. Mr Volwrath fastened her up, and we had to pay a dollar to get her loose. That's the way he does if any range cow gets into one of his fields even if he uses the river for a fence.'

'You don't have to tell me that. I know,' Evaline said.

'Well, you don't have any stock.'

'We have, too. We've got Runt, our pig, and all the chickens, and we might have a nice milk cow before long.'

'I thought you were going to move to town, a high school town.'

'We might if my dad gets a good section job to bid on. He's just waiting for a chance to bid so Lester can go to high school.'

Evaline was troubled at the prospect of moving and was glad to change the subject. 'Say, I wonder if there are any hazelnuts over there this year?'

'We can ride right over and see.' Wilbur turned Tarpaper off the road towards the steep ravine. 'Look along the sides of this hollow and see if there's hazel brush.'

'I see lots of pawpaw bushes,' Evaline said. 'My dad calls them poor man's bananas.'

'I'd rather have real bananas,' Wilbur said. 'Hold on now, I'm going to take Tarpaper right up the side.'

Loose rocks rolled under the horse's hoofs, and Evaline held to the back of the saddle. They rode far into the brush on the steep side of the ravine. 'I just know that little hazel thicket is around here close,' Wilbur said.

'Tarpaper is liable to fall in a place like this. We'd better tie him and get off and walk,' Evaline said.

'He's surefooted as a pack horse. He could make it all right; but if you want to walk, okay.'

They tied the horse to a sapling and climbed single file along the side of the ravine.

Wilbur jumped; for as he parted the vine-matted sumac brush, he stepped into an enclosure and found himself face-to-face with a stranger. Evidently the man had been lying on the ground asleep; for he raised up almost as startled as Wilbur.

Evaline looked over Wilbur's shoulder. She pushed

back the wisp of hair that always got in her eyes. She thought she knew everyone in Middling, but she didn't know this fellow, although she had a feeling she had seen him before somewhere. His face was unshaved, his clothes dirty. The deep line at the bridge of his long nose made him look as if he had frowned most of his life.

'What are you kids doing here?' he growled at them.

'We were just looking for some hazelnuts,' Wilbur explained. 'Have you seen any?'

'No, I ain't. There ain't none here. And if you know what's good for you, you'll clear out right now.'

'It's all right for us to be here,' Wilbur said. 'This is Ab Whiteside's land, and he doesn't care if we get nuts off it. What are you doing here, camping?' Wilbur asked, as he looked around the vine enclosure and noticed a pack on the ground.

'None of your business,' the man snapped. 'Get out.'

'We're not really hunting hazelnuts,' Evaline said. 'We're hunting for an old man. Have you seen an old man?'

The stranger started. 'Who else is looking for an old man? What about him?'

'We're all looking for him,' Evaline explained. 'He had a pack on his back. Have you seen him?'

'No,' the man snarled. He moved closer to his pack as if to shoulder it.

'I know just about everybody that lives around Middling,' Evaline went on. 'There aren't very many. I've even got a feeling I saw you somewhere before. I can't place you though.'

The frown line set deeper in the man's face. 'I'm not bothering anybody up here, but if you kids won't clear out, I'm moving on.' He reached down for the pack at his feet. It was then that Evaline noticed his shoes. They were new, sturdy brogans.

'Now I'm beginning to remember,' she said. 'It was those shoes. I saw you by the spring, just last night it was, but you didn't have those new shoes then——'

With a curse he dropped the pack. 'No, kid, you never saw me before.'

'You didn't have them,' Evaline continued. 'It was the old tramp who had the new yellow shoes, just like those, because he said to me——'

'You saw somebody else. I wasn't around here last night.' The look on the man's face changed. He tried to smile, but it didn't seem like a real smile. 'How would you kids like to make some money by staying here for a few minutes to watch my pack? I haven't got any grub. Ain't there a store around here where I could buy something? I'll pay you when I get back.'

'We've got something else to do,' Wilbur reminded him.

'Oh, now, wouldn't you help a hungry man get some grub?' He tried to smile and speak kindly, but his voice sounded as if it were out of practice in such speaking.

Evaline felt uneasy. 'I don't want to stay here.'

'Maybe there's ways of making you,' the man shouted and grabbed something from his pack.

As she turned to run, Evaline saw a coil of rope. Both children clawed at the tangle of vines and squeezed through passages so small that they held back the man who ran after them. Evaline half-ran, half-fell down the side of the ravine.

It was only ordinary clothes-line rope she'd seen. She didn't know why she ran unless it was the look of fear and hate that she saw flash across the stranger's face. It was something about his new shoes, but she didn't know what it was. If they could just get to old Tarpaper!

The horse shied and tangled his bridle when he heard yelling and crashing in the underbrush. Wilbur struggled with the reins, but his fingers were all thumbs. Evaline worked with the tangle. Her hands flew. She freed the rein just as their pursuer caught up with them.

Wilbur whirled Tarpaper round. For a second, his trampling hoofs blocked the stranger.

Wilbur grabbed the pommel of the saddle, Evaline the back of the seat. They both slid up on the right side of Tarpaper. Mounting on the wrong side was the one thing that made the patient old horse kick. In dodging the kick, the man missed the rein by an inch.

On the steep ravine side, Tarpaper stumbled and went down almost to his knees before he recovered his balance. Evaline trembled and held on for dear life. Curses and a volley of rocks followed them. One rock struck Tarpaper on the thigh and set him off in a dead run.

Brush lashed across Evaline's face. She crouched low behind Wilbur to save her eyes. Tarpaper left the woods and tore across the gypsy campground. Evaline's braids flew out straight behind her. He'll go right across the road and into that barbed wire fence, she thought in panic. But some instinct headed Tarpaper into the road towards Middling.

'Is he still coming?' Wilbur shouted to be heard above the pounding of Tarpaper's hoofs.

Evaline looked back. 'I can't see him.'

'What made that guy so mad?'

'I don't know, Wilbur, something about his shoes. Stop, Tarpaper, whoa! Stop him, Wilbur!'

'I can't stop him,' Wilbur called.

Evaline set her teeth lest Tarpaper's pounding should knock them together and chip them.

Ahead in the road they saw men, each one carrying a shotgun.

'Runaway! Runaway!' Wilbur hollered.

It was Evaline's dad who grabbed Tarpaper's bridle near the bit and held the blowing horse.

Wilbur pointed back up the road. His voice shook. 'We saw a man up the hollow. We went to look for hazelnuts. He chased us and threw rocks at us.'

'Are you sure?' Mr Clark asked. 'We just sent a couple of men up that way. They didn't see a thing.'

'Nothing else would make Tarpaper run away,' Wilbur said.

'He was mean-looking and got awful mad when I said something about his having the same kind of shoes the old tramp had when I saw them by the spring last night,' Evaline added.

Mr Clark looked sharply at Dad. 'Half of you leave the road and go up to the head of the ravine. The rest of us will go along the sides, all except you, Ricker. You see that Miss Evalina and Wilbur get home.'

'But we haven't found Grandpa Stevens yet,' Evaline protested as Mr Ricker started off, leading Tarpaper. 'We've got to hunt for him.'

'My orders from Deputy Sheriff Clark are to take you home,' Mr Ricker said.

'Deputy Sheriff!' Evaline exclaimed.

'That's what Mr Clark is. The regular sheriff came over this morning, lucky the river was low enough to ford, and he deputised Mr Clark until we catch that murderer. You kids might have had a run-in with him.'

Evaline was anxious to get home, home where Mama could fit all the pieces of the puzzle together for her. At the section house, she slid down on the left side of Tarpaper. 'Many thanks, Wilbur, for trying to help me find Grandpa Stevens.'

'I won't be able to look any more now,' Wilbur said. 'Like as not they'll want me for a witness.'

'Oh, Mama!' Evaline cried when she saw her mother in the yard. 'Is it true what Mr Ricker said that one tramp killed another? We saw him, Mama, up in the woods, and he had on the new pair of shoes.'

Mama gasped, then grabbed Evaline with such a hug that Evaline was breathless.

'You don't need to worry none, Miz Stevens. The whole posse is closing in on him,' Mr Ricker said, 'but her and Wilbur was too close to that bad bird for comfort.'

'Mama, we didn't find Grandpa Stevens.'

'The old fellow? Why, he's up at my house,' Mr

Ricker said. 'He's happy as a hog in a mudpond, because he sold my wife a quart of vanilla and enough salve to grease a wagon axle.'

'Didn't he go towards Beaumont?' Evaline asked.

'Didn't get no farther than my house,' Mr Ricker declared.

'Please get Wilbur home. Mrs Bates is worried. Then I'd be much obliged to you if you would get Grandpa Stevens started home as soon as you can.'

Evaline was glad to be in her own house. Even though she was ten years old, she crawled up into Mama's lap.

'Evaline, your eyes are so big they look as if they would roll out of your head,' Mama said.

'Did you see how funny Wilbur looked?' Opal asked. 'You could have knocked his freckles off with a stick.'

'It was terrible, Mama,' Evaline shivered. 'I can still see those big yellow shoes, the stitching and the rivets and all. And that man's hands, they were like a woman's hands—only dirty—like a man's hands who hadn't done any man's work.'

Grandpa Stevens came home soon, carrying his pack. They watched him go into the shed to hide it. He came out humming. Dad came home too, but he wouldn't answer questions for a while.

After the heater fire was lit to take the evening chill off the house, Dad told them what he thought had happened and how it finally ended.

As the old tramp slept, the young one must have stolen his new shoes. He woke, and they fought over

165

them until the young man killed the old one. Then the man hid in the ravine, hoping to get away in the night.

Evaline and Wilbur stumbled on to his hideout. He had hoped to persuade or to force them to stay there until he had another chance to escape, but the children got away. The fugitive gave up when he saw the posse closing in on him. He declared he'd killed the old tramp in self-defence. The sheriff took him back to the county seat, and he would have a chance to tell his story in court.

Evaline studied her shoes, how the leather was curved and sewn to fit her foot. 'I guess it's awful to have no shoes when you need them,' she said.

Dad made a place for her on his knee beside Joe Junior. He said, 'It's worse to have no pity, no mercy. Better to go barefoot through the world than to go without love or mercy.'

A train whistled for the Middling crossing. They were all there in the section house that the trains passed, all of them: Mama, Dad, Grandpa Stevens, Lester, Gertrude, and Joe Junior. And Opal was there too, listening to the lonesome whistle.

12

DAD PUSHED BACK from the breakfast table the better to see the yard and right-of-way, which the early morning light showed white with frost.

'It's cold enough to butcher,' he said. 'There'd be no trouble of meat spoiling before it could be used or cured. I'll speak to Grandpa Malone about coming over and helping me butcher Runt. That pig put on a sight of growth last summer and fall.'

Gertrude had carefully sopped up the yolk of fried egg with a bit of biscuit, but she did not pop it into her mouth. Horrified at Dad's words, she held it in mid-air until she realised that everyone, except Dad, was looking at her. Even he noticed her drop the morsel, slide off the bench, and run from the dining-room.

Grandpa Stevens was first to speak. 'Moon's not right to butcher. If you butcher in the light of the moon, the meat will all shrivel up in the frying pan. 'Twon't be any good.'

'That's so,' Mama agreed quickly, 'the moon's not right.'

'The moon's got nothing to do with butchering,' Dad declared. 'Now let me ask all of you something. Did Gertrude go and make a pet out of that pig in spite of all I told her, right from the start, about that pig being our winter's meat?'

'Yes, she did, Dad,' Opal spoke up. 'She did for sure.

She was out there rubbing that pig with a corncob just about all the time. And she'd talk to that thing, and she wasn't the only one either.' Opal raised her eyebrows and nodded her head towards Grandpa Stevens. 'Every washday when she and Evaline were supposed to empty the water, after we got through washing, they would carry the heavy tubs clear out there to the pen, with water sloshing all over them, and they would put that pig in the soapy water and give her a bath.'

'Did you know they were doing that, Nora?' Dad asked.

'To tell you the truth, Joe, I was so give out after getting a big wash on the line, I didn't pay just a great deal of mind what happened to the wash water.'

'And Gertrude was forever running out to feed that pig,' Opal took up her report. 'Runt got so rotten spoiled. Once she squealed and squealed in the night, and I know for a fact that Gertrude got up and got some potato peels and things and fed her, to make her be still.'

'I guess it didn't do any good to warn her not to make a pet out of Runt,' Mama sighed. 'Honestly, Joe, I don't think I'd relish the meat much myself.'

'It'd be like eating one of the children,' Grandpa Stevens said in a voice quavery with age and near-tears.

'Great heaven above! Can't a man butcher a hog?' Dad picked up his dinner bucket and started for the track. At the door he stopped and looked back at his family. Gertrude's muffled sobs sounded from the bedroom. 'Well, take Runt over to Whiteside's. Mr Volwrath comes there every fall to buy hogs. Maybe he'll buy Runt. I don't suppose you'd object to using the money.'

'Gertrude, Gertrude!' Evaline tried to pull the bed-covers away from her sister's face. 'Listen! We don't have to butcher Runt. Dad said so. We can take her over to the Whiteside place, and maybe Mr Volwrath will buy her when he comes to trade hogs.'

'She'll get butchered anyhow,' Gertrude cried. 'Volwraths have a great big smokehouse to fill.'

'No, they don't butcher all the pigs, Gertrude. Now, listen! Mr Volwrath feeds most of them all winter long on corn. The pigs eat and get fat, and it's a mighty good life for a hog. Why, Volwraths raise so much corn, they have to go around and buy extra hogs to feed it to. Wilbur told me.'

'It's all the same,' Gertrude insisted. 'Mr Volwrath doesn't fatten up the pigs just for something to do.'

Evaline couldn't think of any argument to comfort her little sister. 'Gertrude, you could cry and cry and cry until there was no cry left in you. I don't feel so good either, but you know Mama says where there is life there's hope. Saturday we'll ask Wilbur to haul Runt in his wagon out to the farm. Then we'll just see what happens. How about that, Gertrude.'

Gertrude's face was blotched and red. 'All right,' she said finally in a small, exhausted voice.

When Evaline awoke Saturday morning, it was almost as dark as when she went to bed. The room was chilly too, and she hurried to put on her long underwear so that she could finish dressing by the heater fire in the front room.

169

Sunday mornings when her long underwear was clean from Mama's washboard, boiling pot, and breezy clothes-line, she had no trouble fitting her long black stockings up over the ankle-length underwear legs. Her new, high-topped leather shoes laced up neatly. But, as the days of the week passed, the underwear legs stretched, and she had to fold over a triangle at the bottom of the leg in order to get her stocking to fit smoothly. It took extra time and was a big nuisance; she wished Mama would realise that long underwear was not needed every single day of the winter.

When Wilbur came, Evaline saw he had put high stock stakes on the sides of his wagon. They really weren't needed, for after Runt was loaded she did not try to move about. She braced herself in the jolting wagon on her small, graceful feet. Evaline looked back at her and wondered how anything as big and fat as Runt could get about on such nice little feet. Runt managed better than Miss Finneyfrock, the stylish new Middling teacher, did in her high-heeled shoes, and Miss Finneyfrock was slim as a slat.

Gertrude looked back too, from her place on the wagon seat. 'Runt's got three kinks in her tail.'

'That's a sign of good luck,' Wilbur said.

The sun was out full and bright; and by the time they reached the farm, the frozen ruts of the road softened to mud. Tarpaper pulled right up to the Whiteside barnlot. Shep, the farm dog, barked a greeting. Ab Whiteside was hitching up the buggy. 'Say, what you got there?' he shouted in a voice that could be heard over much of the farm. 'I was told you were in the trading business.' He came over to the wagon to look at Runt. 'Are you sure you're not bringing hog cholera on to my place?'

'Oh, no, I should say not, Mr Whiteside,' Gertrude said. 'She's a terrible healthy pig. She's never been sick. Runt was hand-scrubbed all summer.'

Ab Whiteside ran his hand along Runt's arched back. 'It's a wonder this pig thrived at all—being kept that clean. You destroyed all the growth-making dirt a pig needs. You might have killed her! I guess she was tough, though, because she looks fine.'

'Do you think Mr Volwrath will buy her when he comes to look at your pigs?' Evaline asked.

'Well now, that I couldn't say,' Ab Whiteside admitted. 'We never know when he's coming, but he's due here any time. I'm going to take Miz Whiteside to catch a train at Middling this morning, so I might miss that closefisted customer. I'll leave the trading to you and your Grand-dad Malone in case Volwrath appears. Your grand-dad is better at trading with him than I am. He's got more patience. Don't let Shep follow me.'

Sunrays glanced from spoke to spoke of the buggy wheel as Ab Whiteside reined the horse around smartly and drove from the lot.

Wilbur found a wide cleated plank to prop up at the wagon endgate, and Runt walked daintily down and was turned into the barnlot. Grandpa Malone came from the barn and was met with a volley of questions.

'Hold on! Hold on, now! Let me have a look at this shoat your ma said you'd bring over.' Grandpa Malone pushed his woollen winter cap to the back of his head.

'Look at the red hair on that pig. That's the prettiest I ever saw.'

'That's because Runt's a Duroc-Jersey,' Wilbur explained.

'It just beats me what a fine pig that is,' Grandpa Malone went on. 'I've seen turkeys live on grass-hoppers and lizards, but I've never seen a hog before that thrived on potato peels and dishwater.'

'Lester said if she'd had bran, ship stuff and tankage, it's hard telling what she would have done,' Gertrude said.

'What do you think Mr Volwrath will pay for her?' Evaline asked.

Grandpa Malone threw up his hands. 'They wouldn't know in heaven above. But he'll be here, maybe today. He's been trying to get the Whiteside hogs for nothing for years. I've beat him guessing the last three years. He's out to beat me for sure this year, and he might do it. My luck has run out.'

'I guess so,' Gertrude agreed dismally, 'but how did you beat him other years, Grandpa?'

'I outguessed him on the weight of the hogs. Then I took them to the scales at Middling and found the actual weight. Whichever guess was closest to the real weight was the price paid. Each time, my guess has been nearest right, but he's out to skin us for sure, this year.'

'Why don't you have a scale right here at the farm? Then you'd know what the pigs weigh,' Evaline suggested.

'And take all the fun out of selling pigs!' Grandpa Malone shook his head.

'I remember how it was last year,' Wilbur said. 'I was out here with Lester when Mr Volwrath came. I'll never forget that, because I didn't notice and let Shep in the lot. He chased most of the pigs through the hole under the lot gate, out into the little pasture. We had to go drive them back when Mr Volwrath came.'

'It takes kids to remember everything,' Grandpa Malone said. 'Details escape me now. But I do know Volwrath will want this fine hog you've brought.'

They were so engrossed in admiring Runt that they did not notice Mr Volwrath until he stood with his long arms spread atop the plank fence of the barnlot. He'd left his horse hitched to the house yard fence, and it seemed to Evaline almost sneaking of him to come so quietly up to the barn.

Mr Volwrath's steely blue eyes were shaded by an old black felt hat, banded with a ribbon that time had shredded. Instead of a blue chambray work shirt, he always wore a light-coloured shirt designed for a starched collar. He did not wear a collar, but fastened the narrow neckband with a collar button under an Adam's apple so sharp it seemed it would cut his throat. The usual farmer's work jacket he spurned too, for a heavy sweater which had stretched almost to his knees from the weight of tools in the pockets. The sweater had long lost all its buttons, and Evaline was intrigued at the way he kept it fastened with nails thrust through the knitted yarn.

Mr Volwrath and Grandpa talked and talked—about crops, politics, the weather—about everything except pigs, although they grunted and clanged the lids of self-feeders across the fence.

Curiosity kept the children nearby during the long, aimless conversation. Evaline brought ears of corn from the crib, and they shelled corn while they waited for Mr Volwrath to come to the real point of his visit.

Evaline shelled faster than Wilbur or Gertrude, and it was fun to take off a whole row of grain with the side of her hand. After a time, though, her hands got cold and sore from the rough kernels. She wished Mr Volwrath would talk trade.

Wilbur went over to inspect the lot gate and the size of the hole in the planks at the bottom of it. Then he did an odd thing. In a low voice he coaxed Shep, the farm collie, to him; strode to the pig lot gate and deliberately opened it wide enough to let Shep in. Wilbur's faintly hissed 'Sick 'em' was enough to send Shep bounding at the pigs in a fury of barking.

The pigs squealed and searched for escape from Shep's snapping teeth. Some squeezed through the hole in the bottom of the solid gate at the far end of the lot.

'Ya, Shep, ya!' Grandpa Malone called, but his voice was lost in the confusion of barks and squeals.

Most of the pigs pushed through the hole under the gate. Runt shoved her head through. Then it seemed she was stuck. By pushing with her dainty hind feet, she barely squeezed through. Since Shep couldn't follow, he turned to chasing a half-dozen hogs that were too big to get through the hole and escape him into the larger pasture. Shep, evidently, thought it was his duty to clear the lot of pigs.

Evaline could tell that Grandpa Malone was plenty mad. So could Shep, who was finally called off and ran, tail-tucked, out of the lot. Wilbur looked hangdog too, as Grandpa Malone scolded him for carelessness with a farm gate and for using a trained dog for amusement.

At least, Mr Volwrath's attention was turned to the hogs. He took Wilbur's part and said a little more running would not take much meat off those thin razorbacks.

'Razorbacks!' Grandpa Malone exclaimed. 'Volwrath your eyes are failing. You're looking at top hogs.'

Finally, Mr Volwrath got around to asking if they were for sale.

Grandpa Malone said they might be for the right price. There followed a long, sideways approach to the right price, which Grandpa Malone at last announced was ten cents a pound for hogs averaging a hundred and fifty pounds a head.

Mr Volwrath's steely eyes took on a look of disbelief. He turned and marched away indignantly with his long sweater flapping.

'Now you've made him mad, and he won't buy Runt or any other pig,' Gertrude whispered.

'Just keep shelling corn,' Grandpa Malone advised in a low voice.

Wilbur fidgeted and could hardly wait until Mr Volwrath was out of hearing. He pulled at Grandpa Malone's arm.

'The ones in the little pasture, the pigs that got through the hole, they weigh a hundred and fifty. Six that couldn't make it weigh a hundred and sixty. It was that way last year. I remember. They fill up the hole. I couldn't see any daylight around them when they pushed through.'

Grandpa Malone pushed back his cap and was still staring at Wilbur when Mr Volwrath returned.

'I just came back to tell you that in forty years of feeding livestock, your guess is the most unreasonable I ever heard. Those shoats won't average a hundred and thirty-five, and the market price is only eight and a half cents a pound.'

'No,' Grandpa Malone disputed. 'The six here in the lot average one hundred sixty-five. The ones over there in the little pasture average one hundred fifty-five. That's my final guess.'

Mr Volwrath's final guess was much lower. A price of nine and a quarter cents was agreed upon, and all was to be settled when the hogs were hauled in the big farm wagon to the scales at Middling that very afternoon. They watched Mr Volwrath ride away on the best five-gaited horse in the country: a horse that could walk, trot, canter, run-walk and rack.

Grandpa Malone patted Wilbur's shoulder. 'You've helped me beat him again, four years in a row now! And to think we had an automatic pig sorting machine right on the place and didn't know it.'

Grandpa went off to get the wagon ready for the haul to Middling. Gertrude took a last look at Runt in the hog lot. Evaline could tell that Runt looked special even in with all the others.

Late in the afternoon, Mama sent Evaline to Clark's for flour, oil, and dry beans. Gertrude came along to help carry the load. The girls left the main line and carefully walked the rails that led over the cattle guards to the house-track spur. On Clark's warehouse close to the house track, a torn circus poster flapped in the November wind. Wilbur saw the girls from the depot window and ran to meet them.

'Gertrude! Gertrude!' he called as he ran. 'Runt's saved. Runt's saved!'

'How?' Gertrude asked in disbelief.

'I watched for your grandpa to bring in his load,' Wilbur explained, 'and when I saw him I ran down the hill from my house and helped him drive the pigs out of the wagon on to the scales.

'Mr Volwrath and just about everybody came out of the store to watch Mr Clark weigh the load. You should have seen the look on Mr Volwrath's face when they finished the figuring. Grandpa Malone guessed just two pounds over the right weight, and you might know, Mr Volwrath was way under. So they settled up right there in cash, and your grandpa said for me to tell you that he'd see you got your money.'

'But how was Runt saved?' Gertrude asked.

They reached the big scale that was between Clark's store and the road. The heavy wooden floor of the scale was larger than a barn door. When the children stood on it and swayed, it moved gently back and forth. There was a roof above it to protect the wood from weather, and there was a tiny building beside it that housed the long arm and heavy weights of the balance.

'I'm trying to tell you how Runt got saved,' Wilbur said, as he spread his arms and rocked from one foot to the other to try to set the floor of the scale in motion. 'Your grandpa went into the store with Mr Clark to get the weight slip, and everybody was bragging and bragging on what a good guesser he was. Mr Volwrath began to look like himself again with his eyes all squinty. He pointed to Runt with his stick. He said Runt was a fine Duroc-Jersey hog and that your grandpa had made a mistake and sold her right along with stock hogs. He'd got an extra fine hog for no extra price, he claimed. He told everybody that he was not going to fatten Runt for market but keep her on his place for a brood sow.'

Gertrude jumped up and down on the scale until it shook violently. 'I can just see her, just a-mincing around Volwrath's big farm as good as any stock on the place.'

'Better than most,' Wilbur said.

'She'll never be sent to market,' Gertrude said with satisfaction. 'She'll live on the Volwrath farm and have lots and lots of fine red baby pigs, but she won't ever be rightly a Volwrath.'

13

SLEET RATTLED AGAINST the school window. Even if the room had not been dark, Evaline's eyes burned too much to study. Her head throbbed, and her throat hurt terribly when she tried to swallow. She didn't play during afternoon recess and was relieved when four o'clock finally came. She'd never known the walk home to be so long.

When she came into the front room, Mama looked searchingly at her, then felt her forehead.

'Undress and go to bed, Evaline. You're hot as a fox.'

Later, when Dad was home off the track, Evaline heard Mama talking to him. 'I think we should have the doctor, Joe. Gertrude and Joe Junior are dragging too.'

'Maybe it's just sore throat. You know what doctoring runs into.'

'Yes, but the whole school was exposed to diphtheria a week or so ago. Even Joe Junior went up there to play at recess. Rickers didn't keep their kids home when they were sick. They just keep them home to work when they are well. Miz Ricker tied white rags around their necks and kept them in school as long as they could put one foot in front of the other. I guess there's no doubt they had diphtheria. Miss Finneyfrock didn't know to send them home as Mary Kyle would have.'

After many years of teaching the one-room Middling

school, Miss Mary Kyle had retired. All Middling children, and many adults too, had known no teacher except her. Miss Rebecca Finneyfrock, a girl from Beaumont, had been hired to teach. Evaline had heard Mama say she was only seventeen years old.

Lester went to the store and asked Mr Clark to call Dr Brady, who came that night. He looked at Gertrude's throat, then at Joe Junior's and Evaline's.

He leaned back in the straight chair. 'Well, you've got three with it. How about the rest?'

'Lester had diphtheria when he was four years old, and I think Opal had it easy then, too.'

'They're young, so I guess it won't go very hard with them. They're all under eight, aren't they?' Dr Brady asked.

'Oh, no, Doctor. Evaline here is ten,' Mama explained.

'I wouldn't have thought so,' Dr Brady said as he put a fever thermometer in Evaline's mouth.

The pain in Evaline's throat was dreadful, but far worse was the feeling that she was smothering. She often dropped off to sleep but woke clutching for the good air around her.

Somehow she lost track of days and nights and even of people who came and went. Mama was beside her often. She knew that. Once she noticed Gertrude and Joe Junior playing on the floor by her bed. She wondered how they could feel well enough to play. She didn't know what had happened to Opal, for she saw little of her except when she came to bed at night.

Grandma Malone came with extra butter for Evaline,

and Mrs Shank brought her some soup from the boarding cars. Although it was smacking good soup, she couldn't swallow much of it.

Dad sat by her bed and sometimes Lester was there. She tried to tell Lester about the Hebrew children in the fiery furnace. She didn't realise that her painful efforts to talk sent him running for Mama.

'Mama, Evaline's clear out of her head with fever,' he said. 'You know that oil-burning engine just went by. When it shook the windows the way oil burners do, that woke her up. The flash from the firebox shone right into the room when the engine passed. She talked about the Sunday school lesson, about the fiery furnace.'

Mama stayed for hours beside Evaline, putting cloths wrung from cold water on her head. Dr Brady came that day, but Evaline was too sick to know he was there.

The doctor listened to her heavy breathing. 'Too bad she hasn't a little more strength to fight with, like those two.' He pointed to Gertrude and Joe Junior who were now almost well.

'Oh, she's tough,' Mama insisted, 'tough as a pine knot. And she's gritty too.'

'I hope so,' Dr Brady said. 'But the infection has spread in her throat. If she gets worse, get warm, steamy air for her to breathe.'

That night Mama sat by Evaline's bed as she had done the night before. Dad stayed in the kitchen to tend a big fire in the range which kept water steaming in kettles and in the reservoir at the side of the stove.

Next morning Mama nodded in her chair, but Opal lay awake beside Evaline and watched in the dim light. Evaline struggled but seemed unable to call for help.

Opal cried, 'Mama! Dad! Help Evaline!'

Evaline remembered the kitchen where she gasped for the steamy air. Finally, breathing became easier, and she fell asleep.

It was daytime when she woke. She was on her cot. She saw Ethel, her dish doll, and reached and got her from the nearby dresser.

Each day Evaline felt better. Mama brought patching and sat beside her bed.

'Is diphtheria as bad as flu?' Evaline asked.

'Well, yes and no,' Mama answered puzzlingly.

Evaline thought of the headstones in the Whiteside graveyard. All those were taken by the flu, Grandma Malone once told her. Evaline thought of Mama threatened by the dreadful flu, and tears rolled down her face. Mama wiped them away with the edge of the quilt. 'There now, it's hard to keep a stiff upper lip when you're weak. Say now, a lot happened while you were sick. Miss Finneyfrock and Lawyer announced they were going to get married. Miss Finney-frock has given up the school.'

Evaline felt her rough, parched lips. She had to think for a moment to remember that Lawyer was one of the bridge gang. He had given Mrs Shank the plaster bathing girl. Mrs Shank would be glad, she knew, that Lawyer was to have a wife. Evaline was glad too, that there was no school at Middling; for she did not feel as if she could sit in school all day. Still she knew it wouldn't do to let little kids like Gertrude and Joe Junior grow up to be dumb-bells.

'Won't we have any more school at Middling?'

'You just bet your boots we're having school at Middling, and a rattling good school, too. Miss Mary Kyle is coming back. When she heard Miss Rebecca was fixing to get married, she said she'd take the school again. Miss Rebecca just wasn't cut out to teach.'

'She dressed awful stylish.'

'Yes, right up to snuff,' Mama agreed, 'but she knew herself things weren't right. All people aren't cut out from the same——'

Mama stopped because of the roar of a passing train. Evaline thought of Mama's words. She thought of Opal, who was cut from a different pattern than she was. She knew that. Still, they all lived here in the section house where the trains passed, so they could be different and alike too.

When it was quiet again Evaline asked, 'Who did the work, Mama, while you took care of Gertrude and Joe Junior and me?'

'Opal did. I couldn't have asked for better help. She packed Dad's bucket, did extra washing, and a lot of cooking. She was on the go all the time.' Mama laughed shrilly. 'She was cranky the whole time, but she worked.'

Gertrude came in with more news for Evaline. 'Dad bid on a job at Duncan,' she reported. 'And he might get it.'

Mama made Gertrude stop talking about Dad's bid.

She said they'd better let Evaline rest. Still Evaline wondered about Duncan. It was a high school town.

The first few days she was up, Evaline stayed indoors. For her first walk outside, she bundled up in Opal's outgrown winter coat, woollen tam, scarf, and leggings, as if she were going to the North Pole. She was surprised, though, at how cold it was. Winter winds bent the bare trees. Across the track, she could see the frosted vines and dry cornstalks of the garden. Hills across the river were a dull purple-grey.

When she came home from her first day at school, Dad made a fuss over her and made a place for her on his knee beside Joe Junior. It was crowded but mighty good just to sit there.

'How did school go, Water Skip?' he asked.

'It seemed a hundred miles up the hill. I sat down on a big rock by the path. Wilbur saw me there and wanted to know what was the matter with me. Coming home nobody was cold except me. They all ran, but the wind blew right through me.'

'Do you hear that, Nora? Now's the time to get that cow you've been wanting.'

'Duncan?' Mama questioned.

'No, another fellow got it who'd worked longer for the company.' Dad seemed glum but then made an effort to change his mood. 'Now's the time to get that cow, so that Evaline can have a big glass of milk still warm from the cow. She ought to have that twice a day. Then she'd pick up and get strong in no time.'

'We need a cow. That's for sure,' Mama agreed. 'We need her right now, but a cow's got to have a stable.'

Gertrude came in the back door, shivering with cold. She carried a splint basket of china fragments and battered saucepans. Frosty bits of earth clung to the playhouse utensils. 'Can Joe Junior and me put this stuff in the loft? We're not going to play house until it gets warm again. Then we're going to build a new house with boards from Runt's pen. We're going to use the bluff for one wall.'

Mama stared at Gertrude. 'Joe, like it says in the Scripture, "out of the mouths of babes!" Why, that would be a fine place for the cow stable, out of the wind, right under the bluff where the kids played house. One strong wall to tie to ought to brace up the whole building.'

Dad considered. 'It wouldn't take much to put up a three-sided lean-to out of rough lumber we could get at the sawmill out by Botan's place.'

'Maybe Wilbur could haul lumber with Tarpaper,' Evaline suggested.

Lester had been listening. 'I could help build the shed, Dad. Let me try.'

They all helped. Wilbur hauled the oak planks from the sawmill. Lester put up the framing. Mama advised on the location of the manger and small loft for hay. Evaline wanted to help more than Mama let her, but she did get to drive a few nails as the roofing was unrolled.

When the job was done, they looked at the new stable anchored firmly to the rock bluff. Dad said jokingly, 'Wilbur, got a cow to sell? We've got everything now but the cow.'

'Mr Volwrath might have a cow to sell.'

'He might, but we don't have purebred Jersey money, not after paying the doctor. We'll have to get an old scrub from somebody. If we treat her right, she'll give us enough milk.'

'It's hard to tell what Mr Volwrath brags on more, his cows or his son,' Lester said. 'Mr Volwrath says he taught August Volwrath to work hard and spend little. At the Beaumont Fair, Mr Volwrath and August took nearly all the prizes. They have a blue-ribbon herd.'

'Volwrath cream is so thick it won't pour out of the pitcher,' Wilbur declared. 'I was asked to eat there once, and the cream just fell out of the pitcher in great big gobs. And you should see all the cream cans down at my dad's depot. Volwraths ship the most cream.'

'Yes, and he'd want a right smart of cash for one of his herd,' Dad reminded him.

'He might have one that wouldn't be so dear,' Wilbur persisted.

'That's right, Joe,' Mama said. 'There's no harm in asking the price.'

Dad agreed to go to Volwrath's the next day after work. Evaline and Wilbur begged to go along. They waited after school while the section gang put the hand-car away. They followed Dad's big steps along the shortcut path towards the boat landing. Wilbur broke off a dry stalk of giant ragweed and whacked away with it.

The river was edged in white, lacy ice. The water was a chill grey-blue like the sky. Dad unfastened the boat that everyone used, and they began to paddle across. Evaline wished the river was wider so the boat ride would be longer.

At the Volwrath farm, everything was ready for a long winter. Hay stuck out of the cracks of the big barnloft. Corn showed golden between the boards of the cribs. Fat strawstacks stood near the barn. The woodpile was almost as high as the house. The open door of the woodshed showed rank after rank of split wood.

It was milking time, so Dad went to the barn to find Mr Volwrath. August Volwrath and the Ricker twins carried pails of foaming milk from the barn. It would take a while to get to the question of the cow sale, Evaline knew; so she and Wilbur followed August to the back porch of the farmhouse, where they could hear the cream separator humming.

Steam rose from the warm milk as August poured a pailful into the big metal bowl at the top of the separator. Prune Ricker turned the long handle. He stepped aside to give Wilbur a turn. Wilbur grasped the handle and bent his back without giving the machine a chance to slow down. A wide stream of white milk came from one extended tube of the separator. That was skim milk for the pigs. From the other tube came a thin golden stream. That was cream to be shipped out of Middling in heavy metal cans. Evaline watched that little golden stream while Wilbur turned.

'You want a try?' Prune Ricker shouted above the hum of the separator.

Evaline pushed the handle with all her might, pushed

until she was dizzy, but she could not turn quite fast enough to keep the stream flowing.

'Let me show you.' Prune seized the handle and set the streams flowing again.

'Don't worry about him none,' Wilbur said as they ran from the porch back towards the barn. 'He thinks he's big now, because he works on a big farm.'

'I never thought Rickers would work on this place,' Evaline said.

'Mr Volwrath is making them work out their rent, because they didn't have cash when he went to collect rent for his house they live in. He makes them all work —milking, separating, feeding, bringing up cows—all kinds of chores.'

Dad and Mr Volwrath stood before the stanchion of a dish-faced Jersey cow. She looked very solemn, for her big soft eyes were ringed with black. Her coat was the colour of molasses mixed with butter.

'I'll be honest with you, Mr Volwrath,' Dad was saying. 'We've got forty dollars for a cow, and that's all.'

Nervously, Mr Volwrath stabbed the nail fastener of his sweater back and forth. 'You can have her for forty,' he snapped.

In amazement, Dad reached out and rubbed the head of the gentle cow. 'I can pay now,' he said, and took his snap-top purse out of his overall pocket.

Mr Volwrath drove the cow from the barn. Right away she seemed different now that she was theirs. Evaline patted her great side. She looked back at Evaline with big, sad, black-circled eyes.

Dad asked to borrow a halter and rope to lead her home. Mr Volwrath's generous mood was gone. 'Cut yourself a grapevine,' was his suggestion as he went off about the milking. August did come with a rope and halter and the blunt order to bring them back.

They led the cow down to the boat landing. Gently Dad coaxed her into the shallow ford. While Wilbur and Evaline paddled, Dad led her from the boat.

The days were so short that there was little daylight left when they reached the section house. But Mama saw them coming. Everyone came out to see the new cow: Grandpa Stevens, Joe Junior, Opal, Lester, Gertrude. At Mama's order they all moved and spoke easily so as not to scare the cow. Evaline felt more like jumping and shouting.

Dad spoke with hushed pleasure. 'There's your cow, Nora, a genuine registered Jersey. We'll even get to-night's milking.'

'Well, I never. Why, Joe! How in this world did you get a fine Jersey like her for forty dollars? Run get that bucket, Opal. You know where it is. I scalded a bucket, Joe, just out of hope, but I didn't think you would really come home driving a fine cow.'

'I don't understand it myself,' Dad chuckled and shook his head.

Mama stroked the cow and murmured to her as if she were a baby. Then she stooped down and began to milk. The thin streams of milk hit the tin pail with a ringing sound. Mama milked so fast it sounded like music.

'Want to try?' Mama asked Evaline in a hushed

voice. 'Just an easy down squeeze.' Evaline tried and, sure enough, a very thin stream of milk came from the cow's udder.

'Mama, I'm going to milk as fast as you do, and I'll milk night and morning,' Evaline promised.

'Not me,' Opal said, turning up her nose. 'I'll help with breakfast in the house.'

Milk was high in the pail when Mama finished. 'Now that's pretty good for a cow to give with a lot of strangers around, the first time in a new place,' Mama declared. Arnold rubbed around Mama's legs. 'Well, look who's here.' She poured milk foam off into a little pan for Arnold.

'I'm proud we've got a cow and can pour off milk foam for the cat, just like a regular place,' Evaline said.

'You just bet your boots we can. Say, what's this cow's name?'

'I didn't ask,' Dad admitted. 'When he let me have her for forty dollars, I thought I'd better get out of there while the getting was good.'

'No matter, we'll give her a Stevens name. You name her, Joe.'

'I always liked the name of Thelma. I read a book about a girl named Thelma, and ever since I've thought it was a real pretty name. What do you think of Thelma for a name?'

They all thought the cow would like that name. Evaline was glad their cow was to be named for a girl in a book just as she was.

Wilbur said he'd better go, or his mother would skin

him. He ran down the right-of-way where Evaline heard chat crunch under his feet. She wondered how he knew Mr Volwrath would sell Thelma for forty dollars.

To really know, Evaline would have to have been with Wilbur when he met his father, who was leaving the depot.

'Wait, Dad,' Wilbur called.

'Come on, or we'll both be in trouble for being late for supper.'

Wilbur was glad for the light of his father's lantern. 'Dad, Stevenses got their cow. She's a Jersey from Volwrath's for forty dollars.'

Mr Bates stopped in his tracks. 'You must be mistaken, Wilbur.'

'No, I'm not, and I know why too,' Wilbur continued, as he and his father walked towards the Bates home. 'Ever since Rickers started working out their rent, the twins have been driving up the cows. I could see them across the river when I was out after April. That black-eyed cow was very gentle; so they jumped on her back, both of them, and rode her. Thelma would high-tail it clear through the pasture, for no cow likes to be ridden, especially to carry double. They'd slide off, nice as you please, when they got near the barn. But Thelma was so worked up she wouldn't give much milk.

'Mr Volwrath keeps a milk record on every cow. One day at school, the Rickers told me Mr Volwrath thought that cow was sick. He must have thought he'd better sell her for whatever he could get.'

'Why didn't you tell Mr Volwrath the Rickers were making a pack animal out of his dairy stock?'

'I don't have a whole lot of conversation with Mr Volwrath,' Wilbur said.

'And he was willing to sell Joe Stevens a cow he thought was sick,' Mr Bates mused.

'He sure was.'

'Stevens is the kind of man who might drive that cow right back across the river if he knew why he got it so cheap.'

'Maybe he won't need to know.'

'Under the circumstances, maybe not,' Mr Bates agreed.

14

THE SECTION GANG climbed on the handcar. If Evaline hurried she could ride as far as the depot where Dad stopped for a morning line-up. She pawed through the wraps hung on the pegs by the front door, but couldn't find her winter cap. She grabbed Opal's instead and ran out, calling for Dad to wait.

Wilbur was at the depot, quiet for once as he stood beside the ticket window.

'Number 26, t-w-e-n-t-y s-i-x, to meet Number 9, n-i-n-e at 10:18, t-e-n e-i-g-h-t-e-e-n, at Beaumont, B-e-a-u-m-o-n-t,' Mr Bates spelled out.

Dad and Evaline waited quietly too. Mr Bates repeated a train order on the railway telephone. A mistake could cause a wreck. Dad's line-up, which Mr Bates received by telephone from the train dispatcher, had to be accurate too. It told Dad when to expect extra or delayed trains in the daily schedule. Dad and his gang had to dodge between fast and slow trains and keep the handcar in one piece.

Evaline's reason for coming to the depot was to weigh herself on the platform scale in the freight room, which was cold as a barn. She quickly balanced the beam. It came down with a clang as she jumped off the scale to hurry into the warm telegraph office and report a weight gain of a pound and a half.

'Evaline, you're getting to be an easy keeper, like Thelma,' Mr Bates said and pointed to a stack of bulletins and charts on his desk. 'Lester and I have figured out a balanced ration for Thelma.'

'Mr Ab Whiteside was real tickled we got Thelma from Volwraths,' Evaline said. 'He's supplied her winter feed in return for all the extra work Lester did on the farm.'

'He did plenty,' Mr Bates agreed. 'Now, clear out. I've got a train order to hand up. Don't forget Rule N.'

' "When should you expect a train?" ' Wilbur reviewed the question from his father's railroad rule book.

'Expect a train any time from either direction,' Evaline gave the correct answer as they ran out of the depot and up the track.

Clark's warehouse, beside the right-of-way, caught Wilbur's attention. He stooped to study the building which was set on low posts at each corner. 'Evaline, I'll bet you can't crawl under Clark's warehouse without getting stuck.'

'Oh, I can too! I can do it quicker than you can say Jack Robinson.'

It was awful under there, and Evaline wished she hadn't tried it. The tightest squeeze was under the sill at the very end. She made it, but left Opal's tam pulled off on a nail. Neither she nor Wilbur noticed it as they ran on to the section house.

Mama was in the kitchen, working butter in a big wooden bowl. She pressed moisture from the golden ball of butter with a wooden paddle that Grandpa

Stevens had whittled out of red cedar. As she worked, the ball became firmer. Mama added coarse salt.

'Take off that dirty coat, wash your hands, and you can work the butter,' Mama said. Evaline was very pleased for Wilbur to see that she was trusted with an important job like working butter.

Mama cut squares of wax paper from a roll. Then, with the wooden paddle she filled the butter mould, pressed on its handle, and out on to the clean paper plopped an exact pound of butter.

'Will there be *three* pounds?' Evaline asked.

'Well, now, we'll just see,' Mama said, as she pressed butter into the mould again. 'You just bet your boots there's three pounds and a little pat besides.'

'Three pounds and a pat,' Evaline repeated.

'We only need two pounds a week. We got along on one for years; so looks like we've got butter to sell as well as milk,' Mama said proudly.

'Did you know about the milk, Wilbur?' Evaline asked. 'Thelma gives more than two gallons a day now. It's more than we can keep sweet even in winter; so we sell a quart a day to Miss Mary Kyle.'

Evaline helped Mama wrap the butter. 'Of course you can't expect Thelma or any other cow to keep this up all year long,' Mama explained.

'Her milk will fall off some, but then——' Mama's voice rose, 'we'll have a calf!' Evaline grasped the edge of the cabinet to steady herself for Mama's hard hug.

Opal's shrill voice broke in. 'Where's my tam?'

That day and the next the section house was searched for Opal's tam. It wasn't much in the way of headgear.

Mama had crocheted it from used yarn scraps of all colours, and the bulky pompom showed it was made from ravelled out yarn. Still, it was the only tam Opal had. Evaline knew she'd lost it and didn't find it until Monday when she came from school. There it was, in a half-frozen puddle near the warehouse. A rat must have mauled it. It was ravelled, torn and smelly. Opal took one look at it and said she wouldn't wear it to a dog-fight.

Evaline begged Grandpa Stevens to whittle out a good smooth crochet hook. Wilbur supplied new yarn, which he said his mother had intended to use to make something for Dorothy but hadn't gotten around to. It was a nice old-rose colour. Evaline crocheted as fast as she could. Still it looked as if she wouldn't get that tam done before Christmas.

At Clark's store two new wooden boxes sat on the counter. One held cranberries, one celery, things Mr Clark ordered specially for Christmas.

On the dry goods side were a few dolls and wind-up toys. Evaline didn't see what she wanted to buy at Clark's. She had a silver dollar to spend which Grandpa Malone had given her for pulling through the diphtheria. She wasn't sure that her idea was a good one, so when Dad came in off the track one evening, she asked him.

'Dad, do you think it would be wrong to give a cow a Christmas present?'

Dad considered. 'As I understand it, a cow had a right honourable place at the birth of Jesus Christ, so I don't see anything out of place in giving a beast a gift.'

'I can't get it at Clark's, and I don't want it home-made.'

'Clark's don't carry what I want either,' Lester joined in.

'Well, it's only three days until Christmas, so I guess you two can take the railroad pass and go into Beaumont on Number 34 tomorrow afternoon.'

The next day seemed like a week, but it finally passed. By late afternoon Evaline and Lester got off the train in Beaumont. It was very exciting to be on a trip with her big brother. Evaline had her silver dollar tied in the corner of her handkerchief. They decided to go to Quality Hardware, a store recommended by Wilbur.

Evaline liked hardware stores, for they stocked so many things a person could use. Now, just before Christmas, tinsel was draped over the hammers and wrenches that hung on the wall. Letters fastened to a cord were strung across the width of the store. These were hard to read because they were printed to look as if they were made of ice-covered logs of wood. It took Evaline a while to realise that they spelt out 'Merry Christmas'.

While Lester stopped to look at bowls and baskets on the front counters, Evaline went to the rear of the store. On a back display table among milk pails, strainers, and calf weaners, she found it. She read the inscription, 'Made in Switzerland', stamped on top. She swung the cowbell gently. A sweet-toned note rang out.

She carried it to the front of the store, where the hardware man showed workbaskets to Lester. Evaline tugged at his coat. 'This is what I want for Thelma.'

She swung the bell again. The Merry Christmas sign seemed to vibrate.

'That's a gen-u-ine Swiss bell,' the hardware man said. 'They say those bells have a nice soothing effect on cows, not like the noisy, homemade blacksmith bell.'

'How much?' Evaline asked.

'Sells for one dollar.'

'I'll take it.'

Lester selected a beautiful sewing basket for Mama. The top was decorated with coloured beads and a ring handle.

When they left the store and went out into the winter dusk, Beaumont's Main Street was almost deserted. Evaline noticed streaks of light in the western sky, but the stores they passed were dark in contrast. Most of them were closed, their windows cold black squares or dimly lit by a single bulb.

A few people hurried along the street. 'Everybody in Beaumont must be home for supper or trying to get there,' Evaline said.

'All but this fellow.' Lester patted the wooden Indian that stood in front of the cigar store and stared out across the sidewalk to the railroad switchyard that paralleled Beaumont's Main Street.

Evaline thought she recognised the woman hurrying along the street towards them. It looked like Wilbur's Aunt Annie. She hoped it was, so she could tell Wilbur about seeing her. A torrent of words ended the question. It was Wilbur's Aunt Annie, all right. Orville Bates had been lodging with her since he started high school in Beaumont. Aunt Annie recognised them.

'Well, I declare, aren't you lost so far from home? Come up to Beaumont to find Santa, did you? Well, I'm all ready, what little I do. Of course, I'll come down to Middling on Christmas Day to have dinner at Bates's. Orville went home for Christmas vacation, and he won't be back until after New Year. He's not much company, such a quiet boy, but better than nothing. Sometimes I think it's lonesome for him too at my house. Orville'd be better satisfied if we had another boy staying with us, and so would I, for that matter. Don't say anything to my sister, Miz Bates, but Orville is not very much on work—real work like carrying in wood and taking out ashes, things I expected him to do. Once he gets down to a book, he just don't hear hints nor shouts about work.'

'Well, I'd like——' Lester tried to interrupt.

'If I could find another boy that wanted to board in town and go to high school, and if he was really willing to do the chores I have, well, I could see my way clear to reduce his board by half. That's only two-fifty a week. Of course, I wouldn't make a thing by it. Most boys have hollow legs. You can't fill them up, but still——'

Evaline punched Lester. He finally managed to interrupt and ask if she would consider him as a lodger. She declared Lester to be the kind of boy she wanted. She knew from Wilbur that Lester was a good worker and wouldn't track in mud.

Lester explained that even with the reduced rate for board and room, he would have to confer with Mama and Dad. Ten dollars a month was a lot when Dad made only a hundred.

Wilbur's Aunt Annie agreed. She'd wait to hear. If things worked out, Lester could start boarding at her house after Christmas vacation. She lifted the fur collar of her coat up to the brim of her bucket hat, said she had to get home to see about fires, and was gone.

'Oh, Lester, do you think you can, maybe?'

'Hard telling. I wish we didn't have such a long wait now for Number 47. I'd like to get home and tell Dad and Mama.'

Lester shifted his package from one arm to the other. Evaline thought of the warm kitchen at home, of supper on the table. A sharp, quick whistle sounding over the steady clang of a locomotive bell drew Evaline's attention to the switchyard. Even in the half-light, the man who stood beside the caboose swinging a lantern looked familiar. 'Isn't that Hotbox Barr?' she asked.

Lester studied the freight train a moment. 'It is, and that's the regular local freight, hours late, this time of year. He's about to pull out.' Suddenly Lester grabbed Evaline's hand. 'Come on, maybe we can get to Middling in time for supper.'

Evaline ran and jumped across ties and rails to keep up with Lester. Hotbox Barr signalled the engineer. Then he saw them coming. 'All aboard,' he called.

A puff of steam rose from the engine. A shudder started in the head boxcar, moved back from car to car, and struck the caboose just as Evaline caught the curved grab-iron railing and swung up the steps. Lester followed her. The train moved faster so that Hotbox Barr had to run to catch the grab iron and hop to the rear end.

Hotbox puffed and grumbled. 'You kids deadheading

it for Middling? We'll do well to get you there before midnight. The dispatcher puts us on the sidetrack for a section handcar.'

Evaline braced herself in the aisle of the swaying caboose. She looked above her head at the windowed cupola. 'I'll bet you can skin up into that crow's nest faster than a brakeman,' Hotbox said as he noticed her glance.

The metal toeholds were shined by use. She put her foot on the first one, kept her balance by stepping clear across the aisle to the second higher one. A third jump higher landed her in the left side of the cupola. Lester was right behind her.

Quickly Evaline sat down on the small bench and braced her feet on the opposite one to keep from sliding off the slick leather-covered seat. Two brakemen climbed up as she had but bounded across to the cupola seats on the right side of the aisle, leaving Lester and Evaline a snug place to themselves.

Another brakeman stayed below and opened one of the lockers that lined the walls. Evaline glimpsed rolled signal flags, tall red fusee sticks, lanterns, and oil cans, all neatly stored as the things in Dad's toolhouse.

Hotbox Barr turned up the wick of his oil lamp and sat down at his desk. Above it, on curved spikes attached to the wall were blue train order slips and yellow bills of lading like those on Mr Bates's telegraph desk.

Evaline could hear the low laughs of the men and the murmur of their voices above the clatter of the freight train. The fire in the cannonball stove glowed.

The poker, on its nail behind the stove, swung back and forth to scar a deeper arc into the wooden wall. The smell of Hotbox's pipe and of the coal fire all mingled with the cindery smell of the train.

Evaline cupped her hands round her eyes and pressed her face against the cupola window to see the whole train lurching ahead. Smoke and steam from the engine streamed back.

At the side, dim shapes of houses with lights showed. They became farther and farther apart. Soon only clusters of light showed the farmsteads. Sometimes a light moved as farmers with lanterns finished chores.

A caboose seemed a mighty handy, friendly place. Evaline thought of Christmas only two days away. Then Mama could have her basket and Thelma her bell. Evaline felt bursting happy. She knew Lester must feel happy too. She told him about the tam which she had worked on in secret. He said he was glad she was going to make it right with Opal.

'Opal did a lot for you, Evaline, when you were sick,' he said, 'more than you'll ever know if you wait for her to tell you.'

The busy days passed quickly. Mama got out the lined school tablet and the pencil. She and Dad figured about Lester's schooling. Dad showed them how it added up like a sum. Things to put down were: a little milk and butter to sell, Ab Whiteside's help with feed, Lester's work for part of his board, Mama's sewing money, a calf to sell each year. It added up to an answer. Lester could go to high school.

Miss Mary Kyle talked on the long distance telephone

from Clark's store to the Beaumont High School principal, who said Lester could start late since she assured him Lester was a good student and could catch up with the class. Orville Bates agreed to help Lester.

Christmas Eve they went to bed early, but Gertrude was too excited to sleep. She said she was cold, scared and happy, all at the same time, and begged Opal to let her come to the cot of her sisters.

'Only for a little while until you get over being so silly,' Opal warned.

They could smell red cedar. That meant a tree was being trimmed in the front room. They saw it next morning set up on Mama's sewing machine.

There were oranges for everyone and hard candy with little flower patterns in the middle. Joe Junior had a dancer that jigged when you wound it up. For Gertrude, there was a set of real playhouse dishes. Mama told Opal to look in the clothes closet for her present. It was a woollen serge sailor dress with braid-trimmed collar.

'Chocolate English Walkers.' Lester read aloud the words on the end of the box marked for him. He took off the lid, and there was a pair of dark brown shoes so neat the eyelets for the laces didn't even show.

'Those are for high school, Lester,' Mama explained. 'I picked out some like Orville's.'

'A new coat!' Evaline exclaimed when she opened her package. It was a beautiful dark red coat.

Mama laughed. 'I declare, Evaline, I don't know why you're so surprised. That old coat of Opal's is threadbare, and you've outgrown it besides.'

Mama had knitted mittens for Dad. She tacked soft leather on the palms and covered the backs with thick heavy loops. Dad said you couldn't beat them for cold weather track work.

Evaline noticed the look of pleased surprise on Opal's face when she unwrapped the tam. Then it seemed Opal deliberately tried to look dissatisfied. 'It's an ugly colour,' she commented.

Evaline and Lester grinned at each other.

Grandpa Stevens ignored the tree but greeted everyone with 'Christmas gift' as if he alone remembered the holiday. Little gifts, such as peppermint candy from the last store-bill payment, came out of hiding for him.

After breakfast they went out to Thelma's shed. Evaline was allowed to buckle the bellstrap round Thelma's neck. Then she stroked the cow's great, warm, heaving sides. The bell seemed to please Thelma, or at least not annoy her, as she came out of the stable into the sunshine of a mild Christmas Day.

Wilbur clattered up on Tarpaper. His mackinaw was unbuttoned to show his new cowboy suit. He stayed and played 'Prisoner's Base' and 'Wolf-Over-the-Ridge' until it was time for him to go meet his Aunt Annie. The Stevens family left soon, too, for Christmas dinner at Grandma Malone's.

Evaline couldn't remember a merrier dinner or a better winter day for playing 'Hide-and-Seek' around the yard and barns.

By late afternoon, a chill wind came up, and Dad said they had better start home as they now had chores to do. As they crossed the school ground, Evaline heard

Thelma's bell back in the sheltering woods. She and Lester left the others to drive Thelma home.

Gertrude and even Joe Junior helped carry in wood. Mama did the night milking. Christmas was over. When she went to bed that night, Evaline tried not to remind herself that it would not come again for a whole year.

She woke in the night and heard Dad stirring the fire. A train with its bell ringing pulled slowly through the Middling yard. Snow slanted by the wind blew across the locomotive headlight beam. Evaline looked out at the winter's first snow, which whitened the right-of-way and made the spot on the second sidetrack where Mrs Shank's boarding cars had stood seem lonesome.

Evaline heard the front door open. Dad was going out to sweep deep snow from the switches. The wind blew in around the windows. Evaline snuggled closer to Opal, who moaned a little in her sleep but did not pull away. Far off somewhere a train whistled, and nearby a sweet bell tingled. Evaline thought a section house was a very special place to live.